A GOTHIC COOKBOOK

HAUNTINGLY DELICIOUS RECIPES
INSPIRED BY 13 CLASSIC TALES

Ella Buchan & Dr. Alessandra Pino

Illustrated by Lee Henry

For Dolly, Lucia, and Ramona

Contents

Foreword

"FOOD FUELS THE storytelling," proclaim food academic Dr. Alessandra Pino and writer Ella Buchan in this dark and delightful collaboration. They're right. I learned the narrative power of food while writing my 2021 novel, *This One Sky Day*, its protagonist a master chef haunted in true Gothic style by his dead wife. I swear—food encourages a kind of frenzied delight in writers. What else gives this much sensory satisfaction: in color, light, smell, sizzle, pop, texture, memory?

Buchan and Pino have created more than a generous cookbook; this is a powerful literary discourse on food as meaning. As thirteen Gothic writers inspire over sixty recipes, painstaking research reveals food as the perfect fictive device. Food creates—and is itself the subject of—plot; it characterizes, causing argument and connection. Its preparation and consumption conjure atmosphere, hinting at "something else going on beneath the surface." Food's a comfort when life feels impossible. It is symbolic and social, with "its ability to be weaponized." And whether the food is rich pumpkin Spooky Soufflé, inspired by Shirley Jackson's *The Haunting of Hill House*, or lurking like a champagne-quaffing vampire's fading memories of fresh biscuits in Jewelle Gomez's *The Gilda Stories*, we're invited to inhabit literature in a newly delicious way: read about it, then cook and devour it.

Recipes are inspired by actual dishes in the novels or, more obliquely, born of ideas or feelings. Carson McCullers's *The Heart Is a Lonely Hunter* inspires the Bourbon and Caramel Fudge recipe literally made by one character but also imagines the Red Deviled Eggs another *might* have shared with a sixth-grade friend. Dorian Gray's sartorial taste conjures a recipe called A Button-Hole of Parma Violets. *Dracula* inspires a pink-sauced paprikash over black tagliatelle (Mina's Paprika Hendl). In Toni Morrison's *Beloved*, the eponymous child-ghost has an insatiable appetite, "soothed by sugar"—a devastating irony, as the sugar trade devours enslaved humans for profit—and so the recipes are accordingly bittersweet: Brown Butter–Sugar Sand Cookies, Peppermint Creams, and a vinegary beverage called Washtub Full of Strawberry Shrug.

The read is wonderfully nostalgic for those who've read the Gothic titles—I loved being reminded of Frankenstein's shuffling vegetarian monster and the suspiciously chalky milkshake in Ira Levin's *Rosemary's Baby*—but you needn't have read them all. Pino's prodigious knowledge of Gothic subgenre, married with Buchan's food writing, makes it all fascinating, regardless. As a cookbook, this suits all levels, chatty and accessible. Your crumpets are ready to griddle when the batter is like "just-melted ice cream"; use an oven dish big enough for the chicken "and a little more besides." Fruit for jam is "nicely mushy"; one "pops in" vanilla and when roasting onions gives the pan "a little shake" halfway through. At one point, the authors endearingly tell us there's "no need to worry." Every time I thought, "Oh wait, I don't have that equipment/know that technique," there were swift, easy answers. Spatchcocking a chicken, making bread or ice cream without gadgets, even sterilizing jam jars—it's all here—and with vegetarian and nonalcoholic options too.

The Gothic-lit premise allows Buchan and Pino to create the most outrageously varied fare. From Herb and Cheese Egg-Bread to Stuffed Mushrooms in the Living-Room, from Salmon with Caper Sauce to Real Butter Biscuits with Gravy, there's Greek, French, American soul food, Mexican, and Italian influences. The food goes from the complex and dramatic to the quick and easy—Angela Carter inspires both a three-day prep for A Box of Marrons Glacés (candied chestnuts) and the simply delicious Avocado and Shrimp, Lots of It.

I loved this book as a mission statement for pleasure. Our incessant Western moralizing about food means we often need *permission* to feast. Jane Eyre worries what Rochester will think of her hunger, and while women, she says, need not "confine themselves to making puddings," there is the still-lingering question of whether she can truly be good *and* enjoy eating. In this context, gleeful lashings of cream and sugar and fat and chili, allspice, and garlic are positively transgressive, as she urges us not to nibble crumbs like du Maurier's *Rebecca* but "eat scones with gleeful abandon, as it should be." The recipes are generous and created to be shared and stored.

To use Buchan and Pino's words, from their chapter on *Jane Eyre*, this is a "wonderfully comforting [book] even if you're sitting alone, drunk on porter and gin, guarding a secret incarcerated spouse." So I'm off to bake my first Cherry Clafoutis. How could I resist, reminded as I have been of Oscar Wilde's "cold-as-moon" cherries? Good writing and good food will grab you every time.

LEONE ROSS

Monstrous Meals and Culinary Chills

An Introduction to A Gothic Cookbook

SOME OF THE finest Gothic novels are often not considered Gothic at all. They're wrapped up as romances and decorated with ribbons, roses, and ravishment. And that's exactly what makes them so *very* Gothic.

These stories are cakes smothered in frosting and topped with sugared almonds, yet cut into them and there's a hint of mold. They're apples that might break your teeth—or perhaps poison you. They're sandwiches laced with grit, berries that are a little *too* tart, chocolate mousses with an unsettling chalky undertaste (à la *Rosemary's Baby*).

Often, it's the food that features in these stories, whether devoured by the characters or left, untouched, on their plates, that gives the game away. Much of the food in Gothic tales is there to highlight what *isn't* there, revealing a lack of substance, an absence of nourishment, or a void where domesticity might otherwise live out a snug, cozily contented life. Delicious descriptions throw into relief just how odd and terrifying a situation actually is.

Without the cockle-warming roast on the table, we might not have noticed how cold a scenario has become—or how worrisome the idea is of a certain character wielding the carving knife. Without a plate of cold cuts, untouched by the host but presented to the guest, we (and, in the case of this example, Jonathan Harker) may not realize so early on that there's something just a little *off* about that enigmatic count. And without the jolly picnics and food-filled flights of fancy described in *The Haunting of Hill House*, the hunger of the building might not be quite so starkly, terrifyingly apparent.

This is what our cookbook is all about: identifying the rotten core of the apple and (holding it carefully by the stem) examining it for clues about characters, plot, and social commentary. Just as Gothic literature has traditionally held a dark mirror up to society, we've selected stories that, we believe, hold a shiny serving platter up to moldy morals and hypocrisy.

Our intention here is to pick these tales apart, like tender meat from a bone or artichoke leaves from the heart, to explore what the often-overlooked character—food—might be trying to tell us. Along the way, we take these tasty titbits as the inspiration for recipes to bring these stories into your kitchen.

The Gothic and the gourmet may seem like strange bedfellows (or plate fellows), and of course they are. Yet, in many ways, they're made for each other. The relationship manifests itself on the sepia pages of many novels and short stories in the genre, in subtle—and sometimes not-so-subtle—ways.

Early Gothic novels, starting with Horace Walpole's 1764 *The Castle of Otranto* and Ann Radcliffe's works, including the 1794 *The Mysteries of Udolpho*, describe opulent feasts that reflect excess and almost grotesque wealth while also highlighting some characters' isolation. Others take this further, using consumption and tastes to reflect aspects of the characters' personalities and social standing.

One of the earliest examples, and the first text that features in our cookbook, is Mary Shelley's 1818 masterpiece, *Frankenstein; or, The Modern Prometheus*. Here, food—and especially the creature's plant-based diet—provides a conduit for social boundaries and frames a question: what is humanity, and who is *really* the monster here?

Later, Edgar Allan Poe (not known as a foodie) painted scenes of excessive consumption as the nightmarish backdrop to a tale of the doppelgänger in his 1839 story "William Wilson." The story takes the reader to a carnival in Rome where, after a banquet and free-flowing wine, the eponymous antihero confronts his "enemy" and, by extension, himself.

Elsewhere, food is used to reflect a sense of otherness and to highlight when characters find themselves in strange places. In Bram Stoker's 1897 *Dracula*, for example, Jonathan Harker scribbles reminders to retrieve recipes for his fiancé, Mina, and eats heartily, expressing an appetite that will dramatically diminish as the story progresses.

What we eat can, of course, poison us, with terrible and often fatal consequences. So, in Nathaniel Hawthorne's 1844 short story "Rappaccini's Daughter," Beatrice is "nourished" with poison by her father, so that she becomes a threat to the man she loves. In Charlotte Brönte's 1847 *Jane Eyre*, Mrs. Poole's poison is gin, and her overindulgence allows disruptive influences to break out and challenge the veneer of respectability.

Charles Dickens's stories, which lurk around the shadowy edges of the Gothic, use food to illustrate the starkness of poverty and social inequalities. In his 1843 novella, *A Christmas Carol*, families face starvation while Ebenezer Scrooge dismisses a ghostly presence as an "undigested bit of beef." His 1853 novel, *Bleak House*, meanwhile, employs food as an indicator of social class, holding a lantern up to the dark corners of hidden society. The clergyman, Mr. Chadband, feasts on a tea, including "ham, tongue, and German sausage, and delicate little rows of anchovies nestling in parsley," while poor Peepy Jellyby subsists on (often raw) leftovers and scraps.

The urban Gothic era is also evident in Oscar Wilde's 1891 *The Picture of Dorian Gray*, his only novel. Here, a curse is contrasted with the conviviality of dinner parties and the upper echelons of society, where "more than enough is as good as a feast."

In Daphne du Maurier's 1938 *Rebecca*, characters are fed according to who they are and where they rank. So while Mrs. Van Hopper eats fresh ravioli, her employee—the future Mrs. de Winter—gnaws on cold meat.

Later, in Ira Levin's 1967 horror novel, *Rosemary's Baby*, the titular character is fed and watered by a couple with less than honorable intentions. The neighborly act of sharing ingredients and food is subverted by evil forces at work.

Everyone needs to eat to survive. For most of us, food is associated with company, family, society, and, at its best, comfort and conviviality. Because it's so everyday and universal, food has the fluidity to connect the public sphere with the personal one and to bridge the gap between the "normal" and the uncanny. In short, it's the perfect Gothic device.

If food is able to "uncover" social horrors, what can the food that features in Gothic literature tell us about the characters? What are the authors revealing about the time, and the sections of society, they are writing about? What can food tell us about the society we are living in now?

We don't presume to have the definitive answers, and you may well have different opinions on the texts we're dissecting with our knives and forks. But like the best conversation at dinner parties, we hope to spark some lively debate and, most of all, to make you hungry. Once we have, we're ready to feed you with recipes based on the food in these stories, from traditional dishes straight from the pages of favorite novels to creations inspired by ingredients, themes, and famous scenes.

The proof, friends, really is in the eating.

Things to Know

Some Notes on Our Cookbook

EACH CHAPTER FOCUSES on a different Gothic novel, novella, or short story, and chapters are organized in chronological order by publication date.

A discussion of the food in that text is followed by recipes inspired by the writing, and these are organized in order of appearance in the story. The exceptions are recipes inspired by, or connected to, the text's author.

Throughout, we've been careful to avoid major plot spoilers, while simultaneously scattering just enough crumbs—and providing sufficient context—to enable readers to follow our thinking, even if they aren't familiar with the texts. Of course, you may have read each of our featured stories thirteen times—or you might want to, after discovering how delicious they are.

Portion Sizes

How many each recipe serves is based on a mix of practicality, convenience, and common sense with ingredients (we're not going to suggest you use one-fifth of an egg, for example, so our *Rebecca*-inspired crumpets recipe is based on using one whole egg).

We've also considered the occasion, or occasions, each recipe best suits, from a feast for family and friends to a solitary supper best enjoyed by lamplight.

Then, because we're whimsical like that, we've been guided by the role a particular dish or drink plays in its text. Mick's Sad Sundae, for example, is inspired by a rather lonely scene in Carson McCullers's *The Heart Is a Lonely Hunter*. Sure, you *could* make it for everyone, but a one-person heap of ice cream, chocolate sauce, cherries, and chopped nuts feels more in keeping with the spirit of the moment (and the novel as a whole).

Alternative Ingredients and Adaptations

We may be a *Gothic* cookbook, but that doesn't mean our recipes are blood soaked or even all that meaty. Most either are already vegetarian or vegan or can be easily adapted for plant-based and meat-free diets.

We've included notes and more detailed instructions where required, but here are a few easy swaps that can be made throughout:

- Butter, milk, or cream can all be substituted for the same quantity of plant-based alternatives like nut butter, oat milk, or cashew cream.
- Eggs can be substituted with aquafaba (the water from canned chickpeas or beans like cannellini). Use 3 tablespoons per whole egg, 2 tablespoons per egg white, and 1 tablespoon per yolk.
- For mince or ground beef, use the equivalent amount of plant-based ground meat, finely chopped mushrooms, or cooked lentils—or use a mixture.
- Vegetarian or vegan sausages can also be used in recipes with sausages or sausage meat (for the latter, chop finely).
- Switch mayonnaise for nondairy yogurt; coconut yogurt is a nice alternative for most savory dishes.
- You can also use nondairy yogurt in recipes that call for yogurt, choosing coconut for nutty sweetness or opting for something plain, like oat or soy yogurt, if you don't want to alter the flavor of the dish.
- Substitute date, carob, or agave syrup for honey or (where appropriate) slightly increase the quantity of sugar and skip it completely.
- Use agar-agar or a similar plant-based alternative in place of gelatin.

I

A Vegetarian Monster: Betrayal and Berries in Mary Shelley's *Frankenstein*

FOOD HUMANIZES DR. FRANKENSTEIN'S UNNATURAL CREATION, RAISING QUESTIONS AS TO WHO THE REAL MONSTER IS.

An existential crisis doesn't sound particularly appetizing. Nor does a creature cobbled together from long-expired body parts. Yet this timeless tale of nature and nurture, the pursuer and the pursued, and the created and the creator is a source of discussion worthy of the most salubrious of dinner parties.

The kind that Mary Shelley might have hosted with her husband, Percy Bysshe Shelley, the couple holding court over a table groaning under the weight of glazed meats and platters laden with jewel-hued fruits. Guests glugging ruby wine and contributing bon mots might have included Lord Byron, who was present when the seeds of Mary's 1818 masterpiece, *Frankenstein*, were sown (before the limbs were sewn).

In fact, one of the world's most famous Gothic novels might not exist at all if it weren't for Byron.

Mary Wollstonecraft Godwin (she was yet to marry), husband-to-be Shelley, and fellow Romantic poet Byron were among the luminaries vacationing in Lake Geneva in 1816, which "proved a wet, ungenial summer," according to Mary's introduction to the 1831 edition of *Frankenstein.* Conversation scurried down twisted, tortuous avenues, and after long discussions dissecting ghost stories and musing on the horror genre, Byron had a proposal: they each pen their own terrifying tale.

After days struggling against writer's block, Mary—then aged just eighteen—created her monster after what must have been a pretty terrifying "waking dream." "[W]ith shut eyes, but acute mental vision—I saw the pale student of the unhallowed arts kneeling beside the thing he had put together," she writes in the 1831 preface. "I saw the hideous phantasm of a man stretched out, and then, on the working of some powerful engine show signs of life and stir with an uneasy, half-vital motion."

Whatever nightmare the novel rose from, its themes of exile, misery, loneliness, and guilt elevate it above a simple horror or ghost story and place it firmly in the complex Gothic genre.

Contributing further to its eternal relevance are its much-discussed parallels with the Fall of Man, with frequent quotations from John Milton's epic biblical poem *Paradise Lost*.

Like the fallen angel at the heart of that poem, Satan, the creature didn't ask to be created. Abandoned, rejected, and betrayed by his creator, he becomes the monster others already view him as. But is he *really* a monster? Or is Victor, who plays God by digging up bodies and using science to bring forth life, the real monster here?

The interplay between the characters is at the heart of the novel's moral fogginess, as is the common confusion over the eponymous character, with the creature frequently misidentified as Frankenstein.

Many literary critics have pointed out the sympathetic nature, eloquence, and even innocence of the so-called monster. There's a thin, wavy, and sometimes invisible line between perpetrator and victim. There is one aspect in which this line is drawn quite clearly, if you grab a knife and fork and really dig in—and that's food. If there's any uncertainty when it comes to the creature's innocence—and perhaps whether he should be considered "human"—that doubt might be erased just by looking at his diet.

On the most basic level, the fact that the creature eats familiar foods humanizes him, further raising questions as to the ethics of Victor's experiment. It positions the creature as a sentient being, one we should view as a victim of cruelty simply because he has been brought into a world that would inevitably reject him.

Even more interestingly, he's a vegetarian. Shelley makes much of her character's plant-based diet, using it to demonstrate his empathy with human beings and to show his connection to nature, which appears to be deeper than most people's; he enters his dysfunctional life drawn to the soil, flowers, and nature, longing for a simple rural existence he describes in bucolic terms. He is hungry yet instinctively puts others' needs before his own, hinting at a kind heart. It presents a conundrum for readers to wrestle with: how can a creature so reluctant to kill for food, or even to steal food from others, really be a monster?

The creature's diet highlights his separation from a society of meat eaters while also symbolizing his inherent, if corruptible, goodness. Banished to the wilderness after Victor instantly regrets his scientific experiment, the creature observes a family living in a cabin in the woods. He watches their rituals, which mainly revolve around food: preparing breakfast, gathering around the table, building and lighting fires for cooking, foraging for roots and plants. Their diet, he decides, is "coarse but wholesome." It's simple, uncomplicated by modern society or technology. He follows their example and attunes to the changing weather and seasons.

Moved by observing their interactions and aware of their poverty, he makes a conscious decision to only eat fruit and nuts. He will not steal from them, he vows to himself, because that would leave them hungry.

The softness he shows in these moments makes his murderous rampage—after being once again rejected by his "father"—all the more shocking. Witnessing him gently graze and adopt a lifestyle that eschews killing other animals has endeared us to him. Young William, Victor Frankenstein's six-year-old brother, sees a "hideous monster" who wants to eat him and "tear [him] to pieces." We know better. In the most monstrously human way, the creature kills because rejection and self-hatred have driven him to despair and, eventually, revenge. The only time he kills animals for food is to feed Victor, his creator.

In a desperate, final attempt to be accepted and forgiven, the creature uses his diet as a bargaining tool with his creator. If Victor would build him a female companion, and allow him to be free, he will be happy to subsist on foraged acorns and berries and won't need meat to "glut" his appetite.

Sadly, there isn't such a happy ending for the creature (nor for Victor—nor anyone, for that matter). He is a self-fulfilling prophecy—becoming a "monster" who murders from a very human impulse for revenge, out of anger that he has been judged and rejected by a world he skipped into, innocently and happily as a lamb or child.

His final, heart-wrenching monologue describes the "cheering warmth of summer" and his wonder at the "warbling birds"—and how he was "nourished with high thoughts of honor and devotion." He longed for companionship, for "love and fellowship."

Instead, this once benign, nature-loving vegetarian is left utterly, hellishly alone.

Galvanized Vermicelli

IT ALL STARTED with a strand of pasta in a glass case . . . or at least that's what Mary Shelley's introduction to the 1831 edition of her novel suggests. Sort of. In it, she recalls how Lord Byron and Percy Bysshe Shelley "talked of the experiments of Dr. Darwin . . . who preserved a piece of vermicelli in a glass case, till by some extraordinary means it began to move with a voluntary motion."

She's referring to physician (and grandfather of Charles) Erasmus Darwin's experiments in galvanism, specifically the use of electricity to cause muscle contractions. Taken to its logical, fantastical conclusion, galvanism reanimates the dead.

But was Shelley deliberately misquoting or simply misremembering what she'd read or heard? Was a wiggly piece of pasta *really* the inspiration for her novel? Whatever the truth, her words are the inspiration for our recipe: vermicelli coated with a vibrant green sauce, packed with zingy herbs designed to enliven and electrify.

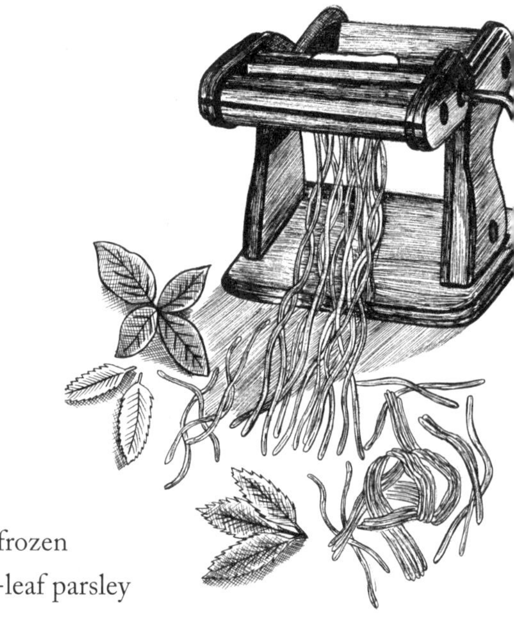

Serves 2

INGREDIENTS

Pasta

1⅔ cups (200 grams) pasta (00) flour
2 eggs
1 tablespoon olive oil
Pinch of salt

Sauce

½ to ⅔ cups (100 grams) peas, fresh or frozen
Handful each fresh mint, basil, and flat-leaf parsley
3 cloves garlic
2 tablespoons capers
Juice of 2 limes
1 green chile
5 tablespoons olive oil
Salt and freshly ground black pepper

METHOD

1. To make the pasta, place the flour in a large bowl, make a well in the center, and crack in the eggs. Top with the olive oil and salt, then, using your fingertips, pull the flour into the center to mix.

2. Lightly flour a surface and tip out the mixture. Knead it for a few minutes to create a smooth, elastic dough. Wrap it in oiled plastic wrap and set it aside (at room temperature) for at least an hour.

3. Turn out the dough onto the floured surface again and flatten it with your palm. Divide it in two pieces and pass each through the widest setting of a pasta machine, folding each time, until smooth. Then continue to pass it through up to setting 6 and finally pass it through a vermicelli attachment.

4. If not using a pasta machine, roll out the dough to around 2 millimeters thick and use a sharp knife or pasta cutter to create fine strands.

5. Hang the pasta to dry for at least half an hour while you make the sauce. To make the sauce, bring a small pan of water to a boil and add the peas. Simmer for around 5 minutes, then drain and rinse them under cold water. This helps to preserve their bright green color.

6. Add the peas and the rest of the sauce ingredients to a food processor (or use a large bowl and hand blender) and blitz to create a smooth, silky sauce. Season to taste with salt and pepper and set it aside.

7. Once the pasta has firmed up, bring a large pan of water to a boil and add a little salt. Cook the pasta for just a couple of minutes and drain.

8. Warm the sauce in a large pan over medium heat, then add the pasta and toss well so each strand is nicely coated.

Acorn Bread

FRANKENSTEIN'S CREATURE ATE acorns raw, freshly plucked from the oak tree or foraged from the woodland floor. It seems his stomach was a little stronger than ours, as unprocessed and uncooked acorns contain tannins that can be toxic to humans. They also have a rather unpleasant, bitter taste, so you probably wouldn't want to nibble on them anyway.

Leave them on the tree for the squirrels (and any wandering, cobbled-together creatures) and instead get hold of some acorn flour to make this dense, crumbly, delicately sweetened bread. It has a texture similar to corn bread and is perfect for sharing. Omit the spices if you prefer something more savory—a pinch of chili flakes will give it a kick and be the perfect complement to a hunk of cheese.

Makes 1 medium loaf

INGREDIENTS

2⅔ cups (250 grams) acorn flour or other nut flour (such as hazelnut)
½ cup (100 grams) superfine sugar
2 teaspoons baking powder
Pinch of salt
1 teaspoon ground cinnamon
Freshly grated nutmeg (optional)
1 medium egg, beaten
1 cup (250 milliliters) milk
2 tablespoons (25 grams) unsalted butter, melted

METHOD

1. Preheat the oven to 350°F/180°C/160°C fan/gas mark 4 and grease a standard loaf pan (approximately 8½ by 4½ inches or 24 by 12 centimeters).

2. Place all the dry ingredients, including a little nutmeg, if using, in a large mixing bowl and make a well in the center.

3. In a medium bowl whisk together the egg, milk, and butter and pour into the well, mixing gradually with a wooden spoon until well combined.

4. Pour the dough (it will be sticky and quite wet) into the prepared loaf pan and bake for around 20 minutes, or until a wooden skewer inserted into the center comes out clean.

5. Remove the bread from the oven and leave it in the pan for around 10 minutes, then carefully remove the loaf from the pan and allow it to cool on a wire rack. (Do feel free to slice and serve it while it's still warm, though.)

Shepherd's Breakfast Bake

WHILE CRUNCHING ON acorns and foraging berries and roots might not be hugely appealing, the "shepherd's breakfast"—which the creature greedily devours, having unwittingly frightened away its preparer—sounds pretty delicious.

That simple platter of bread, cheese, milk, and wine is the basis for our warm, oozily baked savory bread pudding, with layers of sticky caramelized onions. Eat for supper with a crisp salad or serve as a side dish for a brunch or Sunday lunch get-together.

Serves 4 to 6

INGREDIENTS

Caramelized Onions

1 tablespoon olive oil
2 red onions, finely sliced
3 tablespoons balsamic vinegar
2 tablespoons (25 grams) granulated sugar
Glug of red wine
Salt and freshly ground black pepper

Bake

3½ tablespoons (50 grams) unsalted butter, softened
1 clove garlic, finely chopped
Handful of fresh herbs (such as flat-leaf parsley, oregano, tarragon, and rosemary), finely chopped
Pinch of salt
1 medium loaf day-old or slightly stale bread, sliced
1 cup (100 grams) hard cheese (cheddar or a mix), grated
1 cup (200 milliliters) whole milk
2 eggs
1 cup (200 milliliters) heavy cream
1 teaspoon English or Dijon mustard
Salt and freshly ground black pepper

METHOD

1. To make the caramelized onions, place the olive oil in a large pan over medium heat. Add the onions and sauté them for a few minutes or until soft. Add the vinegar, sugar, and wine, increase the heat to high, and cook until the liquid has evaporated and the onions are sticky. Season with salt and pepper.

2. To make the bake, in a medium bowl beat together the butter and garlic, stir in the herbs, and add the salt. Spread this mix over each slice of the bread, then quarter each one into triangles.

3. Preheat the oven to 350°F/180°C/160°C fan/gas mark 4 and grease a 9-inch (23-centimeter) square baking dish (or equivalent size if not square). Arrange a layer of bread on the bottom, top with a layer of the onions, and sprinkle with the cheese. Repeat the layers until the ingredients are used up, ending with the cheese.

4. In a medium bowl whisk together the milk, eggs, cream, mustard, and salt and pepper. Pour the mixture over the bread, pushing down so it soaks up the liquid.

5. Rest the pan for 5 minutes, then bake for 25 to 30 minutes, until puffy and lightly golden.

Berry Bite Squares

OUR CREATURE SPENDS his first few days of existence subsisting on berries and the occasional acorn. He was happy (or at least willing) to do so, but we wonder whether he would have enjoyed these crumbly, delicious fruit-crumble squares a little better.

You can make these with pretty much any seasonal fruit, from apples to rhubarb. Eat for breakfast, for afternoon tea, on a picnic—or as a snack while hiding out in the woods.

Makes around 12 squares

INGREDIENTS

Crumble Topping

1½ cups (175 grams) all-purpose flour
⅔ cups (125 grams) soft brown sugar
1½ cups (150 grams) rolled oats
1 teaspoon ground cinnamon
Pinch of salt
¾ cups unsalted butter, melted

Filling

1 large egg
¾ cup (175 grams) superfine sugar
Pinch of salt
¼ cup (30 grams) all-purpose flour
Zest of 1 orange
1 teaspoon vanilla extract
2 cups (400 grams) berries

METHOD

1. Preheat the oven to 350°F/180°C/160°C fan/gas mark 4. Grease an 8-inch (20-centimeter) square pan with butter and line it with parchment paper.

2. To make the crumble topping, place the dry ingredients in a small bowl, pour in the butter, and mix well.

3. Tip around two-thirds of the crumble mixture into the pan and press down firmly to make a base.

4. To make the filling, in a medium bowl whisk together the egg and sugar, add the salt, then slowly add the flour, orange zest, and vanilla. Stir in the berries so they're fairly evenly coated.

5. Pour the filling over the base, then loosely sprinkle over the remaining crumble mix. (Don't worry if some of the berries are still peeping out.)

6. Bake for 40 to 45 minutes, until golden, and allow the cake to cool completely in the pan before cutting it into squares. The bites should keep well for a few days in the fridge, stored in an airtight container.

Seed
Cake

2

Gin, Tea, and Not Enough Sympathy in Charlotte Brontë's *Jane Eyre*

FOOD IS AN ACT OF KINDNESS, CRUELTY, AND, AT TIMES, DEFIANCE IN BRÖNTE'S GROUNDBREAKING, GENRE-DEFYING NOVEL.

A HUNK OF SPONGE, yellow with egg yolks and dotted with caraway seeds, presented surreptitiously from a drawer. An offer of bread and cheese in place of burned porridge. A mug of hot negus, providing a nervous, cold-handed new arrival with a warm welcome.

Such gestures are woven through *Jane Eyre*. They might seem, on the surface, to be small, rather like Jane herself. They may appear insignificant, a word some might also use to describe Jane. But, as anyone who has read and loved this groundbreaking novel knows, our heroine, at heart, is neither of those things. She's softly strong and subtly steely.

Delve below the surface and those proffered foods—small acts of kindness that signal fellow feeling and warmth—are richly flavored with meaning too.

Let's start with that cake. A classic, fragrant seed cake, it's presented to Jane and her sickly friend, Helen, by Miss Temple, a benevolent yet powerless presence in the cold, damp, hungry world of Lowood School. The girls, famished, feast on their gift as if on "nectar and ambrosia."

That a slice of cake, however generously sliced, bears such significance throws their situation into sharp relief. They are starving and bordering on delirium.

Food is frequently withheld as a punishment. When they do eat, it's in the refectory, a basement space permeated with unpleasant smells. When the cook burns the porridge, it means no breakfast. When Miss Temple offers, in its place, bread and cheese, she is berated by Mr. Brocklehurst, who accuses her of allowing the girls to become accustomed to "luxury and indulgence."

The cake is Miss Temple's rebellion against her position. And, for Jane and Helen, it's a heady taste of a different life in which neither girl, perhaps, belongs.

It sets the scene for many important aspects of the novel, not least Jane's humble yet grimly determined character. She appears to shrink while simultaneously struggling to survive—and succeeding.

Elsewhere, too, food shows our heroine tiptoeing around the edges, never quite belonging either upstairs or downstairs.

Earlier, at Gateshead Hall, Jane takes her (rather scant) meals alone. While Mrs. Reed honors her late husband's wishes by taking Jane in, she also rebels against him by excluding his niece from the breakfast and dining rooms, effectively excluding her from company and society too. For the young Jane, this is a turning point. From that moment on, she is permanently on the periphery, unable to take a seat at the table and, often, not wishing to.

She also judges others through what, and how, they eat and often even describes them via food. So, watching from the staircase, she labels her cousin John Reed a greedy boy who "gorged himself habitually at table."

Sent to Lowood after an encounter with her uncle's ghost, Jane—still a child—considers "never eating or drinking more" and fading away completely. Food becomes an attempt to control a desperate, unjust situation.

At Thornfield she is, once again, caught somewhere between two worlds. And, once again, it's through food that this is demonstrated. Understandably reticent, given her past experiences, she worries that the housekeeper, Mrs. Fairfax, will treat her in a manner similar to Mrs. Reed. The welcome drink of hot negus, a comforting concoction made with wine, lemon juice, and nutmeg, is a pleasant surprise, though her time there doesn't live up to this initial warm promise.

She and Adèle, Rochester's ward and Jane's pupil, are excluded from a dinner party, so Jane grabs some chicken and tarts. Rochester, Adèle later warns Jane, will starve her once they are married. So when she is invited, she refuses to dine with her fiancé. She is suspicious of the offer and perhaps feels once again that she doesn't truly belong. For her, eating is a solitary act; it isn't a social one, and it certainly isn't a pleasure.

Rochester wonders whether she fears he eats "like an ogre or a ghoul," an apt description given his insidiously cruel treatment of her (and in light of a certain secret in the attic). She seems to accept her position simply because she has experienced worse. Yet, at the same time, she is determined that she can improve her lot and even change Rochester. Women (and wives) should not, she muses, in a long passage on gender inequality in chapter 12, "confine themselves to making puddings"—which is exactly what Mrs. Fairfax tasked her with when she first arrived, learning to make "custards and cheese-cakes and French pastry."

Food here, and throughout the novel, provides a misty window into the expectations placed on women, with Gothic conventions such as imprisonment and hauntings highlighted by edible themes. It opens the kitchen door to a discussion on inequality, via Jane's transgression of these traditional rules and boundaries.

Continuing the shift in Gothic fiction that Mary Shelley began, Brontë expands the realm of the domestic Gothic, in which homes replace haunted castles and old churches and in which husbands and family members replace ghosts and demons.

That feminist passage in chapter 12—in which Jane also argues that women "suffer from too rigid a restraint, too absolute a stagnation, precisely as men would suffer"—is, though initially surprising, in keeping with her character: she rebels in small, subtle ways, remaining within the system even while pushing against it. Yet she is also complicit, choosing to marry Rochester regardless—and choosing to view Bertha as a monster rather than a fellow victim of a patriarchal society (a thread picked up, and stitched further into the Gothic tapestry, by Daphne du Maurier's *Rebecca*, ninety-one years later).

Mr. Rochester's secret, locked-in-the-attic wife, Bertha, traveled to England with him from the West Indies, where (it's hinted) he oversaw a plantation presumably worked by enslaved people. At home, he hides Bertha away, declaring her to be "insane."

Ultimately, it's gin, a spirit that, back then, was associated with poverty and marginalization, that allows Bertha to escape. Her keeper, the enigmatic Grace Poole, carries with her a private bottle of gin from which, occasionally, she takes "a drop over-much." It's on one such occasion that she falls into a gin-soaked slumber and Bertha seizes her opportunity to break free and wreak havoc.

She and Jane appear to be polar opposites, with Rochester comparing the "grave and quiet" Jane to the "fierce ragout" and our narrator's clear eyes to "the red balls yonder." Yet both are women trapped by society: Bertha in the most literal sense and Jane by a less visible yet still pervasive oppression. Bertha's situation could also be Brontë's way of following the fate of women in an unequal society to its logical conclusion: to be labeled insane, locked in an attic, and compared to a meaty stew.

Welsh Rabbit with Roast Onion

WELSH RABBIT, OR rarebit, as it's now more commonly known, signals the end of a discussion between Bessie and Abbot on the fate of "Poor Miss Jane." She is, they conclude, to be pitied—or would be, if only she had a more pleasing countenance. Ultimately unmoved by the fact that Jane (who is eavesdropping from her bed, far from sleep) is to be sent away to Lowood School, the pair declare that they could just fancy this classic supper dish "with a roast onion."

It's so much more than posh cheese on toast, especially topped with shallots that have been roasted to sticky, caramelized perfection.

Serves 2

INGREDIENTS

2 shallots, halved lengthwise
2 tablespoons olive oil
1½ tablespoons balsamic vinegar
½ cup (120 milliliters) brown ale
1¾ tablespoons (25 grams) unsalted butter
3 tablespoons (25 grams) all-purpose flour
1¼ cups (150 grams) mature cheddar, coarsely grated
1 teaspoon English mustard powder
1 tablespoon Worcestershire sauce
1 tablespoon finely chopped chives
2 large slices sourdough bread

METHOD

1. Preheat the oven to 390°F/200°C/180°C fan/gas mark 6. Place the shallots in a roasting pan. Drizzle over the olive oil and vinegar, then roast for 15 to 20 minutes, checking halfway through and giving the pan a little shake. The shallots are ready when they're soft and caramelized. Set them aside.

2. Gently warm the ale in a small saucepan over low heat, then set it aside while you make a roux: melt the butter in a medium saucepan over medium heat until it foams, then stir in the flour and cook for a further minute.

3. Gradually whisk in the warm ale, a ladle at a time, for a thick, smooth sauce. Add the cheese and, switching to a wooden spoon, continue to stir. It will become like a thick paste.

4. Add the mustard powder, Worcestershire sauce, and chives, stirring to combine.

5. Preheat a grill to medium-high. Meanwhile, lightly toast the bread and arrange it on a baking sheet, then spoon on the cheese mixture, spreading so it's not quite at the edges.

6. Place the bread under the grill for a few minutes, keeping watch, until it's golden brown. Serve with a dressed green salad and perhaps a glass of leftover ale.

A Kindness of Seed Cake

IT'S A SIMPLE yet significant gesture: a yolk-yellow sponge, dotted with caraway seeds and swaddled in paper, removed tentatively from a drawer and presented like the rarest treasure. To famished Jane and her fading friend, Helen, nibbling on the seed cake is like feasting on "nectar and ambrosia."

The importance of this small act of kindness by Miss Temple is amplified in the context of a cold, cruel world in which children are given scant food and, often, nothing to eat at all.

Our recipe for "a good-sized seed-cake" is adapted from Hannah Glasse's 1805 Nun's Cake, which used a magnificent thirty-five eggs. We recommend slicing and serving it generously, rather than squirrelling it away in a locked drawer.

Serves 10 *to* 12

Ingredients

1⅓ cups (300 grams) butter, softened
1¾ cups (350 grams) superfine sugar
½ teaspoon orange flower water
3 medium eggs plus 3 extra yolks, beaten
1½ tablespoons caraway seeds
2⅓ cups (300 grams) all-purpose flour, divided
1 teaspoon baking powder
Pinch of salt
¼ teaspoon cinnamon
Zest of 1 orange

METHOD

1. Preheat the oven to 320°F/160°C/140°C fan/gas mark 3. Grease and line an 8-inch (20-centimeter) round, high-sided cake pan.

2. Place the butter and sugar in a medium bowl and beat together with a handheld whisk, or mix in a stand mixer until pale. Then, continuing to beat, add the orange flower water and gradually add the eggs and yolks.

3. Toss the seeds in 1 tablespoon of the flour and set them aside—this helps them to integrate better into the cake, so they're less likely to sink to the bottom as it bakes.

4. In a large bowl mix together the remaining flour, baking powder, and salt and slowly add the wet mixture, beating until well combined. Fold in the seeds, cinnamon, and orange zest.

5. Pour the mixture into the prepared pan and bake for up to 1½ hours, checking after an hour, until a wooden skewer inserted into the center comes out clean. Cover loosely with foil if it starts to look too dark—you're looking for an even golden color.

6. Allow the cake to cool in the pan for 20 minutes or so before turning it out and cooling it completely on a wire rack.

A Little Hot Negus

JANE EXPECTS TO be received at Thornfield with "coldness and stiffness." Instead, she is welcomed with a flurry of concerns about her cold hands and need for sustenance. In Gothic literature, of course, comfort often comes before a chill.

The drink chosen to bring some color to her countenance and heat to her hands is a hot negus, made with wine, lemon juice, nutmeg, sugar, and hot water. It was originally created by Colonel Francis Negus in the early eighteenth century and was a popular cold-weather libation throughout the Georgian era, falling from fashion during Victorian times.

We've based our recipe on the original, with some tips from Isabella Beeton, though we'll overlook the recommendation in her 1861 *Book of Household Management* to serve it at children's parties.

If you want an alcohol-free version (that *is* suitable for kids), use cranberry and/or apple juice, adding a couple of drops of bitters for complexity and reducing the sugar to taste.

Makes 1 cocktail

INGREDIENTS

½ cup (100 milliliters) tawny port or juice (if making a nonalcoholic version)

Juice of ½ lemon

2 teaspoons granulated sugar

Freshly grated nutmeg

¾ cups (200 milliliters) just-boiled water

METHOD

1. Warm a heatproof cup or mug by half filling it with boiling water. Leave it for a few minutes, then pour out.

2. Place the port into the warmed cup, then add the lemon, sugar, and nutmeg, to taste, and stir well.

3. Top up with the just-boiled water, stir again to dissolve the sugar, and allow it to cool a little before drinking.

Baked Sago Pudding with Mango Compote

GRACE POOLE, BERTHA'S keeper, once again features in a brief yet significant food scene in the novel. She refuses to eat with the other servants and instead takes a tray upstairs with her, balancing a pint of porter and just "a bit of pudding." We assume that the pudding refers to sago pudding, mentioned just afterward.

Made with a starch from the heart of palm plants grown in Southeast Asia and with a texture similar to tapioca, sago has roots in South Africa's Muslim community, known as Cape Malay people, and its mention in the novel hints at Rochester's colonial, slave-owning background.

It can be soaked and simmered into a kind of porridge or baked like a rice pudding (the traditional English style). We've gone for the latter, as featured in Hannah Glasse's 1747 *The Art of Cookery Made Plain and Easy*. Its warm spices make this a wonderfully comforting dish, even if you're sitting alone, drunk on porter and gin, guarding a secret incarcerated spouse.

You should be able to find sago pearls in health food stores or online, or you can use tapioca pearls as an alternative.

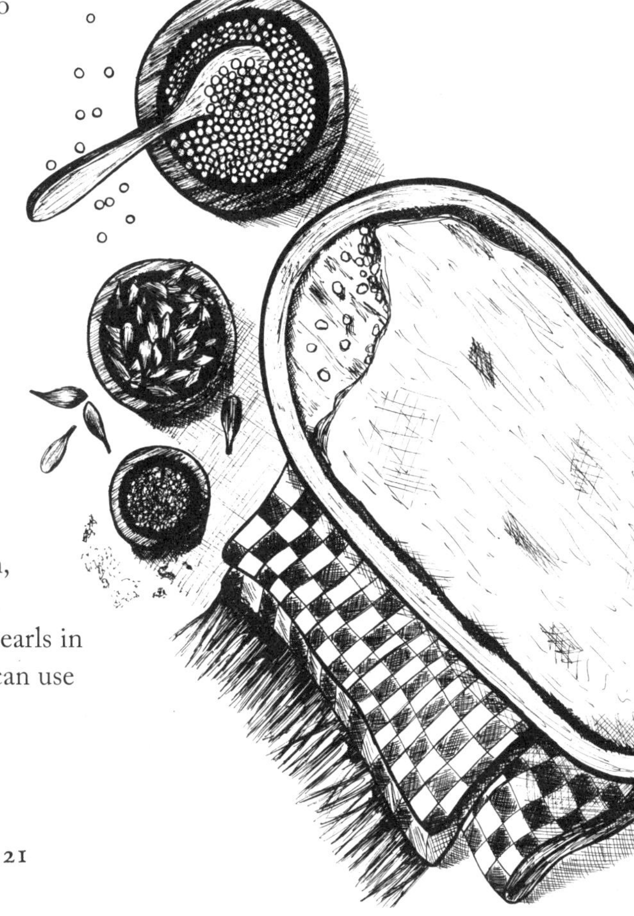

Serves 6 to 8

INGREDIENTS

Pudding

8.8 ounces (1⅓ cups or 250 grams) sago pearls
4 cups (1 liter) milk
2 tablespoons (25 grams) granulated sugar
1 cinnamon stick
1 cardamom pod, lightly crushed
½ teaspoon dried ginger
⅔ cups (150 grams) butter
4 eggs, beaten
2 tablespoons sherry (optional)
⅔ cups (100 grams) currants, sultanas, or a mix

Mango Compote

1 cup (250 grams) fresh, canned, or frozen mango
1 tablespoon granulated sugar
Pinch of dried ginger

METHOD

1. Preheat the oven to 320°F/160°C/140°C fan/gas mark 3. Grease a 9-inch (23-centimeter) square baking dish.

2. To make the pudding, place the sago in a sieve and rinse well with water. Place it in a large saucepan with the milk, sugar, cinnamon stick, cardamom pod, and ginger.

3. Over medium heat, bring to a boil, reduce the heat to low, and simmer, stirring regularly, until the sago is plump and the mixture is thick, like rice pudding (around 15 minutes).

4. Remove the pan from the heat, fish out the cinnamon stick and cardamom pod, then add the butter, stirring well to mix.

5. Beat in the eggs, stir in the sherry, if using, and the fruit, and pour into the prepared dish. Bake for 45 to 50 minutes, until the pudding is firm with a slight wobble to the touch and golden on top.

6. Meanwhile, to make the compote, place the mango, sugar, and ginger in a small saucepan and bring to a boil over medium heat, then reduce the heat to low.

7. Simmer, stirring frequently, for around 10 minutes, or until the sugar has dissolved and the fruit is nicely mushy. Blend the sauce or pass it through a sieve for a smoother, pourable consistency or keep it chunky, like a spoonable jam.

8. Spoon out portions of the warm sago pudding and serve with a generous spoon of compote.

Mrs. Poole's Gin and Tonic Cake, aka Bertha's Escape

Seldom seen, rarely heard, and often talked about, Grace Poole has one job: to keep the first Mrs. Rochester, Bertha, under lock and key. Alas, she has a habit that often enables the incarcerated woman to escape her quarters and roam the halls: a penchant for a particular juniper-infused spirit.

This cake pays homage to this fascinating character—and the liberating power of gin.

Serves 8 *to* 10

INGREDIENTS

Cake

1⅓ cup (300 grams) unsalted butter, plus extra to grease

1⅔ cup (300 grams) superfine sugar

6 medium eggs

2½ cups (300 grams) self-rising flour

½ teaspoon baking powder
Finely grated zest of 4 limes
½ cup (100 milliliters) gin

Drizzle Syrup

1 cup (200 grams) superfine sugar
¾ cup (200 milliliters) tonic water
2½ tablespoons gin

Buttercream

2 cups (250 grams) powdered sugar, sieved
7 tablespoons (100 grams) butter, very soft
Juice and zest of 1 lime
1 tablespoon gin

Icing

¾ cup (100 grams) powdered sugar
Dribble of gin
Juice and zest of ½ lime

METHOD

1. Preheat the oven to 350°F/180°C/160°C fan/gas mark 4. Grease and line a pair of 9-inch (23-centimeter) layer cake pans. Place the butter and sugar in a large bowl and beat together with a handheld electric whisk (or use a stand mixer) until pale and fluffy—around 5 minutes.

2. Gradually add the eggs, beating well after each one.

3. Fold in the flour, baking powder, and lime zest, followed by the gin. Divide the mixture between the two pans and bake for 30 to 35 minutes, until a wooden skewer inserted into the center comes out clean (don't worry about holes, as you'll need to make these for the drizzle anyway).

4. While the cakes are baking, to make the drizzle syrup, gently heat the sugar and tonic water in a small pan over low heat, stirring often, until the sugar dissolves. Turn up the heat to high and boil for a minute. Then remove the pan from the heat, mix in the gin, and set it aside.

5. As soon as the cakes come out of the oven, use a skewer to stab holes across their tops. Drizzle over the syrup. Leave them, still in their pans, to cool on a wire rack.

6. To make the buttercream, add the sugar gradually to the butter either in a stand mixer, or if using a handheld whisk, in a large bowl. Add the lime juice and zest and gin so it reaches a spreadable consistency. (You can add more liquid or sugar as needed.)

7. Carefully remove the cooled sponges from their pans and spread the buttercream on top of one. Sandwich with the other.

8. To make the icing, gradually mix together the powdered sugar with the gin and lime juice, adjusting the dry or wet ingredients until you have a consistency like crème anglaise (it thins quickly, so go slowly). Drizzle this over the sandwich cake, decorate with the lime zest, and allow it to set before serving.

3

Gothic Gourmands and Bitter Sweets in Wilkie Collins's *The Woman in White*

GLUTTONY, GREED, AND THE GROTESQUE ARE ROLLED TOGETHER LIKE SWEETMEATS IN THIS EXTRAORDINARY STORY, CONSIDERED BY MANY TO BE THE ORIGINAL "SENSATION" NOVEL.

WILKIE COLLINS COULD be considered something of a maverick, though he fell short of his contemporary (and friend) Charles Dickens when it came to critical acclaim.

Collins's novels addressed social issues in a different way, using multiple narrators to create suspense while twisting and playing with Gothic tropes, from grand, decaying homes to dastardly villains. These elements combined to form a new genre: sensation fiction. At its core is a characteristic that places it firmly under the broader Gothic genre: the power to play on readers' emotions and nerves. It keeps you on the edge of your seat and, at times, threatens to push you right off it.

The Woman in White, serialized in 1859 and published as a book in 1860, is widely considered the first such novel, with a creepy cast of undesirables from all echelons and dark corners of society. Food features so heavily throughout, from oppressively adhered-to mealtimes and awkwardness around the dining table (often tipping over into anxiety) to sweets used as enticements, that it becomes part of the cast.

What characters eat, how much they eat, and how they eat are all used as indications of personality, while also revealing underlying tensions and (rather more blatant) gender inequalities. Carving a boiled chicken is considered a manly duty, while the novel's gluttonous villain, Count Fosco, devours fruit tarts with a seemingly insatiable appetite, creepily comparing sweets to "the innocent taste of women and children."

The intricate web of a plot spins out from a chilling meeting between Walter Hartright, our hero of sorts, and the eponymous woman in white, who evokes such a visceral reaction that "every drop of blood" in Walter's body is "brought to a stop" by the seemingly gentle gesture of a hand on his shoulder.

As the plot thickens (and twists), it seems that it isn't so much the woman (Anne Catherick) herself whom we should fear but what she represents.

In Collins's novel, and in mid-nineteenth-century England, women are preyed upon and consumed. Unscrupulous, and even outwardly scrupulous, men pluck what they desire, like bonbons from a box, only to discard them when they have served their purpose. Women are the targets of unwanted, and particularly creepy, attention. Murder plots are hatched against them. They're imprisoned, whether in the trap of a suppressive marriage or, more literally, sectioned in an asylum.

Married women's rights would have been fresh in the author's mind: the Matrimonial Causes Act, allowing civil divorce for the first time, was passed in 1857, two years before the novel was serialized. Women were still unable to own property under English law; until 1882, anything that could be considered "belongings" was passed from father to husband. And being wrongly confined to an asylum was a very real fear for women at this time.

The novel's themes and unconventional characters could have been influenced by Collins's own rather bohemian lifestyle. He lived with his mother but "kept" a long-term lover, Catherine Groves, nearby. When he eventually moved in with Catherine, he set another woman up in a house around the corner—going on to have three children with the latter.

So he danced on the edges of acceptability and respectability: the ideal perspective, then, from which to pen a Gothic novel subtly exposing the hypocrisies and injustices of society.

Food is one of the devices he uses. As Mrs. Catherick, the conniving and rather cold-hearted mother of the woman in white, Anne, so wonderfully puts it: "My hour for tea is half-past five, and my buttered toast waits for nobody." Lives are casually destroyed with little if any regret; mealtimes, on the other hand, must not be messed with.

Walter is heading to his new position as drawing master at Limmeridge House with the promise of "gorging English teas and lunches and drinks of foaming beer, all for nothing." The description, by his friend Pesca, conjures images of conviviality and community. It also suggests a level of consumption bordering on the grotesque, while the last two words—"for nothing"—add an unsettling, rather ominous note.

Once at the house, with its dark corridors and decaying wings, Walter gets some measure of its inhabitants through food and dining habits, from the sister who is confined to her room and being served a "restorative tea" to the reclusive Mr. Fairlie, who eats alone. He is warned off some foods ("that cold ham at your elbow") and forced to endure painful silences at the breakfast table, where the first meal of the day is eaten "in the chill air, in the dim light, in the gloomy morning silence of the house."

Walter may be the novel's hero, with a mission to rescue Laura—the beautiful heiress and, on the surface at least, classic damsel in distress—from a dastardly plot, but one other character looms large throughout: that eerie epicurean, Count Fosco. One who at first may appear to be a mere sideshow, bringing lurid comic relief from the main plot, is key to the events. He lurks, somehow, on every page, just as he does over the shoulders of women and girls, tempting them with boxes of sweetmeats.

Fosco's character and intentions are revealed through his appetite and tastes (and via the "vicious cockatoo" that perches on his shoulder). Here is a man of earthly pleasures, one who will consume whatever he pleases, making no allowances to social norms or politeness.

His taste for sweet things, especially, gives him away as a man who aims to possess, defile, and ultimately destroy innocence, rather than (as Walter's aim appears to be) to protect and preserve it. His sharp-witted tongue is coated with sugar, and his pockets are filled with bonbons and sugarplums.

The latter are especially telling. Used by the count to lure women, sugarplums were nothing to do with plums at all, really, aside from perhaps their shape. They were a type of sugar-coated confection, with layers of sugar forming a shell around nuts, seeds, or dried fruit. To talk with one's mouth full of sugarplums was to talk with sweet, and most likely insincere, words.

Fosco is also a connoisseur of tarts. He doesn't discriminate, being equally fond of the sweet, loaded with fruit and consumed with a jugful of cream, and savory, ideally with a "much crisp crust." His appetite seems superhuman, playfully hinting that he is not quite what he seems—and that, even if a sweet tooth "is the innocent taste of women and children," his motives are far from innocent.

Chicken Poached in Wine

BOILED CHICKEN CAUSES some lengthy discussion when, in part one of the novel, Walter Hartright sits for luncheon at Limmeridge House, having already endured an awkward and rather chilling breakfast. First, does Mrs. Vesey prefer it to cutlet or not? Second, is Mr. Hartright *really* "devoured by anxiety" to carve the bird?

He might well be anxious to devour this tempting boiled chicken, which has been slowly poached in wine for tender, butter-soft meat and a flavor-packed stock.

Serves 4

INGREDIENTS

1 tablespoon (15 grams) butter
2 onions, peeled and quartered
2 celery sticks, medium sliced
2 carrots, medium sliced

2 cloves garlic, peeled and gently crushed with the heel of a knife
2 cups (500 milliliters) white wine
2 cups (500 milliliters) chicken stock
1 medium whole chicken
2 sprigs fresh thyme
1 tablespoon roughly chopped fresh tarragon
1 teaspoon allspice berries or cloves
Salt and freshly ground black pepper

METHOD

1. Place the butter in a casserole dish that's big enough for the chicken (and a little more besides) over medium heat. Once melted, throw in the onions, celery, carrots, and garlic. Cook, stirring, for a few minutes, so the onion is soft and almost translucent.

2. Turn up the heat and add the wine so it sizzles and spits a little. Follow with the stock and then place the chicken in the pot, underside facing upward. It should be submerged, so add more stock if needed.

3. Add the herbs and the allspice, season with salt and pepper, and bring the mixture to a boil.

4. Reduce the heat to low and cover with a lid. Simmer for around an hour, then remove the dish from the heat and leave (still covered) for 15 to 20 minutes.

5. Carefully remove the chicken using two large spoons or forks and place it on a carving board or plate. Loosely cover it with foil.

6. Drain the stock into a large clean saucepan using a colander. Reserve the vegetables (removing the allspice berries) and set aside.

7. Simmer the stock, uncovered, over medium to high heat for around 20 minutes, or until it's reduced by around half. Throw in the vegetables for the last few minutes.

8. To serve, ladle broth and vegetables over the carved chicken.

Chocolat à la Vanille Bonbons

Creepy as he may be, Count Fosco does have impeccable taste, as demonstrated by these bonbons. The little sweetmeats—nestled in a pretty little inlaid box and proffered "as an act of homage to the charming society"—are morsels of pure pleasure.

Makes around 26 bonbons

INGREDIENTS

8 cups and ¾ tablespoon (125 grams) unsalted butter, softened
4 cups (500 grams) powdered sugar, sifted
3½ tablespoons double cream
1 teaspoon vanilla extract
⅓ cup (75 grams) dark chocolate
Finely chopped nuts, shredded coconut, or dash of liqueur (optional)
½ cup (100 grams) dark chocolate, to decorate (optional)
½ cup (100 grams) white chocolate, to decorate (optional)

METHOD

1. Place the butter in a large mixing bowl and beat it with a wooden spoon until smooth, or use a stand mixer with a beater attachment.

2. Add the sugar, a spoonful at a time, and continue beating to mix. It will start to look a little crumbly, but there's no need to worry.

3. Add the double cream and vanilla and beat once again until well combined and smooth. Divide the fondant mixture between two medium bowls.

4. Meanwhile, bring a small pot of water to a simmer. Place the dark chocolate in a small heatproof bowl set over the pot to melt, stirring until silky, or place the chocolate in a microwavable bowl and heat it on full power for 20 seconds at a time, stirring and repeating until fully melted.

5. Mix the melted chocolate into one of the bowls containing half of the fondant, either beating well for a uniform color or folding through for a marbled effect. (This is the time to mix in any additional ingredients, if you like.)

6. Cover both bowls and refrigerate them for at least 3 hours, then shape the fondant into balls, measuring out 1 tablespoon at a time and gently rolling between your palms. (You can also make them smaller, if preferred.)

7. Line a plate or tray with parchment paper, place the finished bonbons on top, and return them to the fridge for at least half an hour.

8. If decorating with chocolate, first melt the white chocolate, following the method in step 4.

9. Using tongs or your fingers, carefully dip the dark chocolate bonbons (leaving the rest to one side) in the white chocolate so that half is covered, replacing them on the parchment paper, chocolate side up, as you go.

10. Melt the dark chocolate following the same method and use this to half cover the remaining bonbons, following the steps above.

11. Return all of the chocolate-dipped bonbons to the plate or tray and place in the fridge to set for a further hour.

12. If you're keeping your bonbons naked, they can be enjoyed right away or will keep in the fridge for up to 3 days. You can also freeze them and bring them back to room or fridge temperature as required.

Fosco's Favorite Fruit Tart

There's no need to devour this fruit tart with a "whole jugful of cream" à la Count Fosco—because the base is layered with a wonderfully rich yet light crème diplomat, crème pâtissière folded with cloudlike Chantilly cream. Topped with berries, or any other fruit you happen to have (or fancy), it's pretty much guaranteed to satisfy anyone's "taste for sweets."

Serves 8

INGREDIENTS

Pastry

1¾ cups (220 grams) all-purpose flour
1 tablespoon superfine sugar
Pinch of salt
7 tablespoons (100 grams) butter, fridge cold and cubed
1 egg
2 tablespoons water, cold

Crème Diplomat

1¼ cups (300 milliliters) whole milk
1 vanilla pod
3 egg yolks
1½ teaspoon cornstarch
¼ cup (50 grams) superfine sugar
1¼ cups (300 milliliters) double cream
1 tablespoon powdered sugar
2 cups (400 grams) mixed berries, to assemble

METHOD

1. To make the pastry, place the dry ingredients in a large mixing bowl and rub the butter in with your fingertips until you have something resembling fine breadcrumbs.

2. Add the egg and water and mix together in the bowl using your hands. Flour a surface and turn out the dough. Knead to form a smooth ball. Wrap the dough in plastic wrap and place it in the fridge for around an hour.

3. Preheat the oven to 350°F/180°C/160°C fan/gas mark 4. Butter a 9-inch (23-centimeter) round, loose-bottomed tart pan and dust it finely with flour. On the floured surface, roll out your chilled pastry so it's large enough to slightly overhang the pan.

4. Use the dough to line the pan, allowing it to spill over the sides. Prick the base a few times with a fork, then cover it with parchment paper and fill with ceramic baking beans or dried pulses.

5. To blind bake (precook without the filling) the pastry, place it in the oven for 20 minutes, then remove the paper and beans and return it to the oven for 10 to 12 minutes more, until nicely golden but not brown. Remove the pastry shell from the pan and leave it to cool on a wire rack while you make the crème diplomat.

6. To make the crème diplomat, put the milk in a medium saucepan and scrape in some of the vanilla pod's seeds before popping the pod in too. Bring the milk to a boil, remove the pod, and set the pan aside.

7. Whisk together the egg yolks, cornstarch, and sugar in a large jug and pour in around half of the still-hot milk mixture, whisking well to combine.

8. Pour this back into the pan and, over medium heat, continue to whisk for a couple of minutes. Swap for a wooden spoon and stir as it thickens—it should be like a dense custard, more spoonable than pourable.

9. Transfer the crème diplomat to a large clean bowl, cover closely with plastic wrap (to prevent a skin forming), and set aside.

10. In a large bowl whisk the double cream with the powdered sugar so it forms soft, velvety peaks. Whisk the crème diplomat once again, so it's nice and smooth, then—with a spatula or wooden spoon—fold in the whipped cream.

11. Spoon this into your cooled pastry case, smooth the surface, and pile on the berries. Slice it and serve immediately or keep it in the fridge for a couple of days.

Sugarplums

Sugarplums do typically involve sugar, but (confusingly) they don't traditionally include plums. There's some debate as to where the name came from, with many food historians believing it's due to the confection's shape, typically round or oval, like a plum.

At their simplest, sugarplums were items from dried fruits to whole nuts and even seeds coated in a clear shell of hardened sugar syrup or caramel. At their trickiest, they were encased in layer upon layer of that syrup—and coating individual fennel or caraway seeds in caramel is no easy task.

Today, they're often made in a more truffle-like form, with dried fruits, nuts, and seeds blended together, shaped into balls and rolled in sugar.

We've gone for something of a hybrid: marzipan, dyed violet and rolled around a macadamia nut, then dipped in caramel to form a shiny, sweet coat with just the right amount of crunch. They're perfect for presenting as a gift (ideally, in a less creepy fashion than our dear Count Fosco).

Makes a dozen "plums"

INGREDIENTS

½ cup superfine sugar, sieved, plus more for dusting
1 cup (100 grams) ground almonds
Squeeze of lemon juice
1 egg yolk
Drop of violet food coloring (optional)
12 macadamia nuts, hazelnuts, or Brazil nuts

Caramel

1 cup (200 grams) superfine sugar
½ cup (100 milliliters) water

METHOD

1. Place the sugar in a medium bowl, add the almonds, and stir to combine. Add the lemon juice and egg yolk and, using your hands, mix until it forms a rough ball.

2. Sprinkle a board with a little sugar and tip out the dough. Continue to knead until smooth.

3. Flatten the ball with your hand and drop on the coloring, kneading again to mix it through the paste. (You can transfer the marzipan back to a bowl at this stage, if you're worried about dyeing your surfaces.)

4. Divide the ball into a dozen pieces, each a little smaller than a golf ball.

5. Press a macadamia nut into each piece and roll it so the marzipan forms an oval (plumlike) shape around it. Line a baking sheet with parchment paper and set these aside on the sheet. Allow them to dry out for 2 to 3 hours. They should feel firm to the touch and slightly hardened.

6. Now, to make the caramel (do this only once the "plums" are ready), fill a large bowl with cold water and set it aside.

7. Add the sugar and water to a small saucepan and stir over low heat until the sugar has dissolved. Turn the heat right up and boil, not stirring, until it turns a golden color and reaches a temperature of 340°F/170°C. (Use a sugar thermometer for the best results; if you don't have one, drop a small amount into a glass of cold water. If it forms a ball you can fish out, it's ready.)

8. Plunge the bottom of the saucepan into the bowl of cold water, then remove.

9. Working quickly, gently pick up each "plum" using two spoons or forks and toss it in the caramel, then set each back on the lined baking sheet as you go.

10. Leave these, uncovered, for an hour or so, to set completely.

A Nice Tart for Dinner

IMAGINE BEING "PAST sixty, and fond of pastry," exclaims Count Fosco's hardworking cook, Hester Pinhorn. It's harder to imagine *not* being, and actually his penchant for pastry is one of the count's more endearing qualities.

It gets a little creepier when he compares fruit tarts to females, but we'll set that to one side while we consider this dish: a savory tart inspired by an unsavory character.

So desperate is he to have a "nice tart for dinner" that he pecks away at "Mrs. Cook," suggesting that he gather produce from the market to fill a pastry case. It must have a "much crisp crust, my dear, that melts and crumbles delicious in the mouth."

This leek and cheddar tart is rich, creamy, and lusciously packed into an herby shortcrust pastry case. It can comfortably serve up to six people with some buttery new potatoes and vegetables on the side. Or if Count Fosco is coming to dinner, six tarts should comfortably serve one guest.

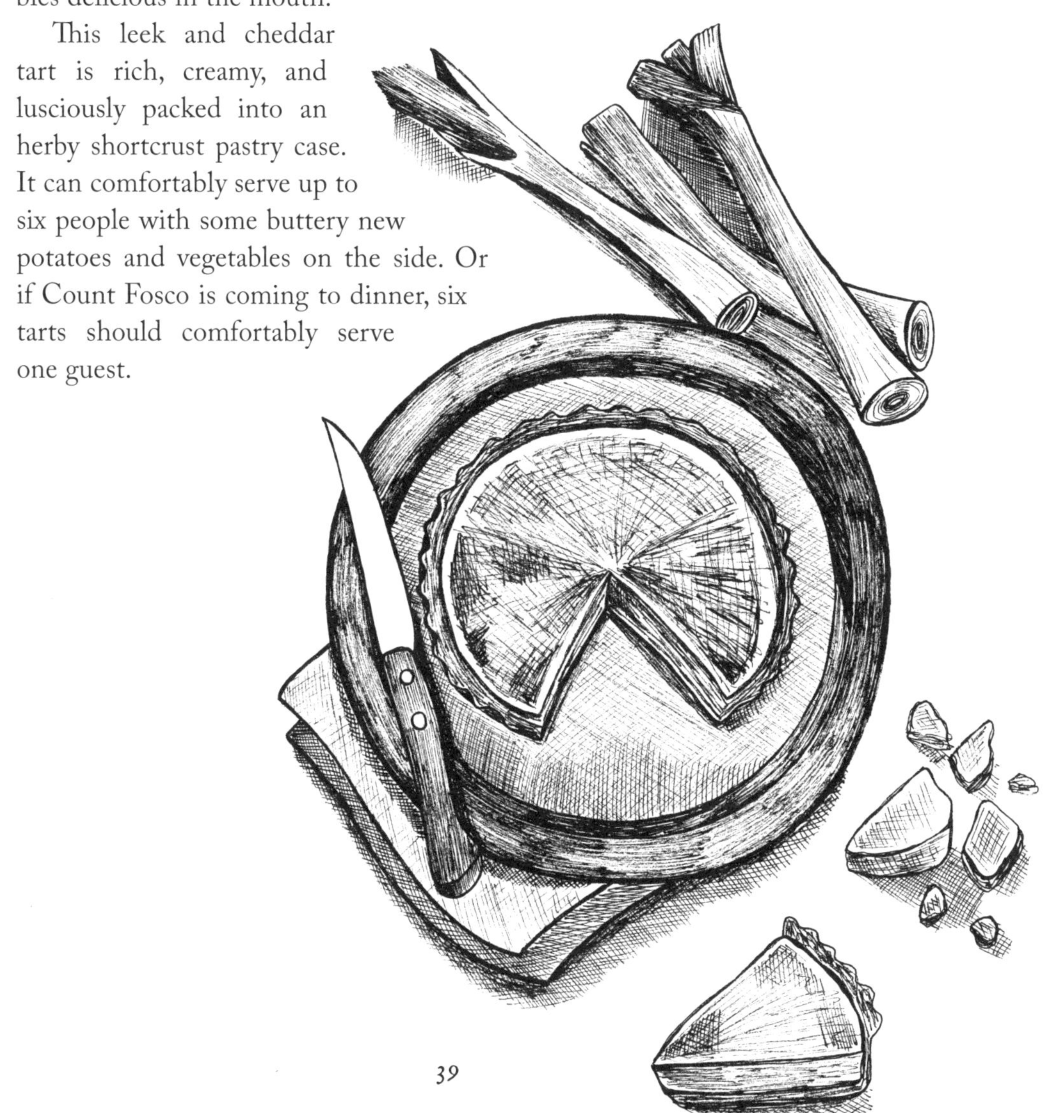

Serves 4 to 6

INGREDIENTS

Pastry

1⅔ cup (200 grams) all-purpose flour, sieved
Pinch of salt
1 teaspoon dried thyme
1 teaspoon dried oregano
½ cup (125 grams) butter, fridge cold and cubed
1 egg yolk, beaten
3 tablespoons cold water, divided

Filling

1 tablespoon (15 grams) butter
3 medium leeks, washed and sliced into 1-centimeter-thick rounds
Salt and freshly ground black pepper
1¼ cups double cream
4 egg yolks
1 cup (100 grams) mature cheddar, grated, divided

METHOD

1. To make the pastry, place the flour into a large mixing bowl and add the salt and herbs, giving it a mix with your hands. Rub the butter into the dry ingredients with your fingertips until you achieve a texture like rough breadcrumbs.

2. Make a well in the center and add the egg yolk, along with 1 tablespoon of the water. Using your hands or a spatula, gradually incorporate with the dry ingredients while adding the remaining 2 tablespoons water, a trickle at a time, until it forms a firm dough. (You may not need all of the water.)

3. Wrap the pastry in plastic wrap or place it in a covered container and refrigerate it for half an hour. (You can refrigerate the pastry for up to 2 days, removing it from the fridge around an hour before the next step.)

4. Butter a 9-inch (23-centimeter) round, loose-bottomed tart pan.

5. Flour a surface and roll out the chilled pastry, so it's sufficient to line the pan with a slight overhang. Use a knife to trim the edges and chill again in the pan for half an hour, while you make the filling.

6. To make the filling, melt the butter in a medium-sized saucepan over low heat, then add the leeks and season with salt and pepper.

7. Sauté for a few minutes, so they're beginning to soften and have released some liquid. Cover the pan and cook the leeks for 10–15 minutes, until nicely soft. Remove the pan from the heat and allow the leeks to cool.

8. In a medium bowl beat together the cream, egg yolks, and two-thirds of the grated cheddar. Season with salt and pepper and add the cooled leeks, mixing well.

9. Preheat the oven to 350°F/180°C/160°C fan/gas mark 4. Remove the pastry case from the fridge and prick the base a few times with a fork, then line with parchment paper and ceramic baking beans or dried pulses.

10. Bake for around 15 minutes, then remove the paper and beans and bake for a further 10 minutes.

11. Remove from the oven, then spoon in the filling and scatter over the remaining ⅓ cup cheese.

12. Return to the oven for 40 to 45 minutes, until the pastry is nicely golden and the filling is just set with a slight wobble.

13. Allow the tart to cool for around 10 minutes before carefully removing from the pan to slice and serve.

COVENT GARDEN

4

Conspicuous Consumption and Cold Hearts in Oscar Wilde's *The Picture of Dorian Gray*

WILDE'S NOVEL USES FOOD AS A MIRROR FOR GREED, DECAY, AND A DIFFERENT, ALL-CONSUMING BRAND OF HUNGER THAT ULTIMATELY DESTROYS OUR ANTIHERO.

CHERRIES BECOME SINISTER in Oscar Wilde's prose. They're offered to Dorian, rather mysteriously and more than a little creepily, by a "white-smocked carter" at Covent Garden market, with no charge. Dorian eats them "listlessly," discerning, somehow, that they were plucked at midnight. They taste of the moon, imbued by its coldness.

Everything about these cherries reflects the eponymous character's mood: sad, bittersweet, deeply unsatisfied, and as chilly as that shimmering satellite in outer space. Having just rejected his love, Sybil, because she's a bad actor, he attempts to find comfort—or perhaps something else nameless and ultimately unattainable—in the beauty that surrounds him, from the fragrance of the flowers (compared to a painkiller) to the violet hue of chimney smoke. It doesn't really work.

His dejected disinterest in food and the complete lack of enjoyment he takes in its consumption are also reflective of his rejection of the corporeal—which, as this scene suggests, isn't exactly bringing him the satisfaction he had hoped. Being an aesthete and giving himself over to a higher form of art, in which eating for pleasure might perhaps be viewed as vulgar, is proving to be rather a bore for Monsieur Gray.

Wilde's haunting, humor-laden novel is peppered with references to the edible, though the actual food is rarely described in any detail. It lurks in the background and in the shadows and sits, barely touched, on a silver tray.

Again, it represents a physical enjoyment that Dorian rejects, with a literal distaste for "the crude violence of disordered life."

Still, he's hungry for all of that and rather dehydrated too—demonstrated in a scene at a party, where every glass of champagne he imbibes leaves him thirstier still. So he lurks around the edges of life, in all its beautiful, ugly chaos and crudity, watching others eat and drink, observing traders at a food market, and never venturing far from the periphery.

He is a walking artwork, a "gracious shape of art," who is unable to truly live, and the biggest tragedy is that it's a tragedy of his own design. It's escaping into art—Dorian's greatest wish—that dampens and eventually destroys any desire within him. He is perfect—and perfectly unhappy.

At a dinner party, "plate after plate" is sent away without Dorian taking a single taste. His lack of appetite doesn't go unnoticed. As the "chaud-froid" is passed around, Lord Henry comments on how "out of sorts" he seems. That the paradoxically hot-cold dish bears witness to this doesn't seem coincidental, especially in light of those cold-as-the-moon cherries. Chaud-froid, in French cuisine, is similar to dishes prepared with aspic; typically, a warm sauce with added gelatin was used to glaze cold chicken or ham.

Dorian himself could be described as chaud-froid (though, as the story wears on, he is increasingly *froid*). His aesthetic appearance and extravagant dress suggest joie de vivre while, inside, he is *misérable*. He moves through a sea of warm, well-fed bodies while his soul is trapped in a dusty, drafty attic.

Decadence and desire, greed and gluttony may well be classic Gothic tropes, but Wilde holds a mirror (or perhaps a paintbrush and canvas) up to reveal a different world: one in which a society fueled by conspicuous consumption becomes all consuming.

Wilde even uses a culinary analogy to comment on the connection between food and art, particularly in the context of the superficial circles Dorian dances around. The "possession of a good chef," he says, is of more value than respectability. "Even the cardinal virtues cannot atone for half-cold entrées."

Yet even the hot, and hot-cold, entrées go largely untouched by our Dorian. It's all for show.

Dorian's lack of culinary indulgence reflects his aesthetic ideal of becoming a higher being who can live without constant nourishment. His half-hearted nibbling on chilly cherries, and his continued seeking out of society, indicates a will to live without having to consume and to experience desire without the burden of having to fully inhabit a body, with all its base functions. He is drawn to everyday life and consistently disappointed in it.

Once freed from the disruption of corporeal existence, he embarks on the pursuit of pleasure. But his frantic pursuit of sensation is accompanied by a progressive emotional and physical numbness, which is mirrored by the food: the way it tastes to him (cold, unsatisfying) and the dwindling amounts he even attempts to eat. The more Dorian strives to experience anything at all, the less he is capable of it: "But I seem to have lost the passion, and forgotten the desire."

The edible creeps into the novel in other ways. There's the name of the fateful portrait painter, Basil Hallward, who initially fails to draw out the true flavors of his subject. Once Lord Henry has managed to entice Dorian's curiosity, Basil begs Dorian to "stop and dine with [him]." Dorian, at first hesitant, opts to dine instead with the elaborately dressed lord, attracted to his finery and beauty.

Wilde delves back into cuisine to demonstrate the duplicitous personality of Dorian, who (for once) seems to enjoy eating his "light French breakfast," declaring the day to be "exquisite" and feeling "perfectly happy." This contrasts with the fate of his first love, Sybil, cruelly rejected by him the day before.

There's a connection, and a contradiction, between food and death, highlighted by the morning meal and the breaking of the fast, bringing life to a new day. There's another happy breakfast the morning after a brutal murder, when Dorian is awoken from a peaceful sleep with a "cup of chocolate." As he sips this rather innocent, even childlike, morning drink, he reflects contentedly on being free of pleasure and pain.

Dorian has become completely indifferent to his sins, accepting his trade of soul for beauty. The sweet innocence of his warm drink serves only to further highlight his malevolence and coldness—or should that be *froideur*?

Cherry Clafoutis

Cherries can hardly be eaten listlessly when they're baked into a classic clafoutis, a rustic French dish that was popular with the Soho set in nineteenth-century London. We recommend a heaped serving of this wonderfully tart yet cozily comforting puffed-up pudding whenever you're suffering an identity crisis. Or even if you're not.

Serves 6 to 8

INGREDIENTS

⅔ cup (75 grams) all-purpose flour, divided

1¾ cups (400 grams) canned pitted cherries, drained; 2½ cups if fresh or frozen

2 tablespoons blanched slivered almonds

1 tablespoon kirsch or amaretto (optional)

4 medium eggs

½ cup (100 grams) superfine sugar (reduce to ⅓ cup [75 grams] if using canned cherries)

Pinch of salt

½ cup (125 milliliters) whole milk

½ cup (125 milliliters) double cream

1 teaspoon vanilla extract

Powdered sugar, for dusting

METHOD

1. Preheat the oven to 350°F/180°C/160°C fan/gas mark 4. Butter a 9-inch (23-centimeter) square oven dish and lightly dust it with 1 tablespoon of the flour. Place the cherries and slivered almonds in the dish, scattering them so they cover the bottom, then sprinkle with the kirsch, if using.

2. In a medium bowl whisk the eggs with the sugar and gradually add the remaining flour and the salt.

3. In another medium bowl whisk together the milk, cream, and vanilla and gradually add this to the batter, whisking to combine until smooth.

4. Pour the mixture evenly over the cherries and almonds, then pop the pan in the oven and bake for around 35 minutes, or until set in the middle and golden and puffy around the edges. Cover loosely with foil if it seems to be browning too quickly.

5. Dust with powdered sugar and serve warm, with light or whipped cream, or allow it to cool before dusting and slicing into portions—it's equally delicious.

Jade-Green Piles of Vegetables

FOOD AND EATING are often a convivial contrast to Dorian's growing malaise in the novel. In one descriptive scene, following his cruel dismissal of Sybil, in light of her lack of acting talent, Dorian wanders around Covent Garden, observing all walks of life and, among other goods, "huge jade-green piles of vegetables."

It's the inspiration for our warm jeweled salad, a vibrant heap of green vegetables dressed in a tangy mix of mustard, lemon, and herbs. This is a lovely side dish for a roast dinner or barbecue and goes rather well with our Perfect French Omelette with Wild Mushrooms (page 49).

Serves 2

INGREDIENTS

2¾ cups (200 grams) broccoli, cut into small florets
1 tablespoon olive oil
⅓ cup (50 grams) peas, fresh or frozen
2 cups (50 grams) salad leaves (such as spinach, arugula, or watercress)

Dressing

1 tablespoon Dijon mustard
1½ tablespoons extra-virgin olive oil
Zest and juice of ½ lemon
Salt and freshly ground black pepper
½ tablespoons finely chopped fresh chives
½ tablespoons finely chopped fresh flat-leaf parsley

METHOD

1. Preheat the oven to 350°F/200°C/180°C fan/gas mark 6. Place the broccoli in a roasting pan and add the olive oil, tossing to evenly coat. Roast for around 15 minutes, or until tender and lightly charred on the edges, then remove the pan from the oven and cover it to keep warm.

2. If using frozen peas, boil them for 5 to 6 minutes, drain, and quickly rinse under cold water (this helps to keep them vibrantly green).

3. To make the dressing, add the mustard to a small bowl and gently whisk in the oil and lemon juice. Keep whisking until the oil starts to emulsify and thicken the dressing, so it's still just a little runny. Add more oil if needed and season to taste with salt and pepper.

4. Toss the broccoli, peas, and salad leaves in a large serving bowl, pour over the dressing, and toss again to combine. Sprinkle over the herbs and lemon zest and serve.

Perfect French Omelette with Wild Mushrooms

French cuisine features heavily in the novel, reflecting the fashions of Victorian London and the upper echelons that our antihero moves within. Dorian is served an omelette as part of a "light French breakfast," and its placement on the table signals the shuttering of his momentarily happy mood (and the window).

It's more to do with the portrait than the dish, mind you—done correctly, to a perfectly even, sunny yellow, it should only lift your spirits, whether eaten for breakfast, lunch, or supper.

Serves 1

INGREDIENTS

2 tablespoons (30 grams) unsalted butter, divided
1 cup (75 grams) mixed wild mushrooms, wiped clean and roughly chopped
½ clove garlic, finely chopped
½ tablespoons finely chopped fresh flat-leaf parsley
Juice of ½ lemon
3 eggs (the fresher, the better)
Salt and freshly ground black pepper
½ tablespoons finely chopped fresh chives, to serve

METHOD

1. Place 1 tablespoon of the butter in a medium nonstick frying pan to melt. Add the mushrooms and gently cook over medium-high heat for around 5 minutes, shaking the pan occasionally, until nicely golden.

2. Add the garlic and cook for a further 2 to 3 minutes. Make sure the garlic does not color or burn, as this will make it very bitter. Remove the pan from the heat and stir in the parsley and lemon juice before setting aside.

3. Crack the eggs into a small bowl and gently beat them until the yolks and whites are fully combined. Season well with salt and pepper.

4. Add the remaining 1 tablespoon butter to a clean nonstick frying pan and heat gently over low heat, swirling to evenly cover the base. Once the butter has melted, keep the pan at medium heat and pour in the eggs.

5. Gently move the pan back and forth while keeping it over the heat. At the same time, use a spatula to gently pull the egg mixture from the edge of the pan into the center, allowing the egg to then run into the gaps. Keeping the egg mixture moving will ensure even cooking and prevent the omelette from coloring.

6. Continue scraping into the middle until the omelette is mostly set but slightly runny in the middle.

7. Turn off the heat and spoon the mushrooms into the center of the omelette. Gently tilt the pan with the handle pointing upward and, with a spatula, fold the omelette downward to the center. Hold over your plate and gently tilt the pan so it's completely vertical, allowing the omelette to roll out.

8. Gently tuck any escaped mushrooms under the omelette (if you want a neat look), sprinkle with chives, and serve.

A Cup of Hot Chocolate on a Tray

Dorian slumbers with the serenity of one who has sold his soul to the devil, waking happily to yet another breakfast brought to his bedside. He stretches into the day with a smile—until the events of the previous evening tiptoe into his consciousness with "silent, blood-stained feet."

Even a "cup of chocolate" brought to him on a tray can't keep thoughts of his dark deeds at bay. If it's anything like this proper Parisian-style hot chocolate, though, it could help ease the most troubled of minds. It's made with proper chocolate for a rich, velvety, and satisfyingly thick texture.

Makes 1 cup

INGREDIENTS

⅔ cup (150 milliliter) whole milk

1 teaspoon brown sugar

½ vanilla pod, split (optional)

Pinch of cinnamon or small cinnamon stick (optional)

⅓ cup (75 grams) dark or semisweet chocolate, finely chopped

Pinch of sea salt flakes, to serve

METHOD

1. Place the milk in a small saucepan and add the sugar, vanilla, and/or cinnamon, if using. Warm over low heat, stirring occasionally, until the sugar has dissolved and the milk is hot but not boiling.

2. Remove from the heat and fish out any aromatics. Whisk in the chocolate until well combined.

3. Return to low to medium heat and bring to a simmer, whisking constantly until it's at your desired thickness (a few minutes for a lovely silky, velvety texture that coats the back of a spoon).

4. Pour the drink into a small cup and sprinkle on a tiny amount of flaked sea salt. Garnish with the cinnamon stick, if used.

A Button-Hole of Parma Violets

DORIAN'S EXQUISITE DRESS sense is one of the many ways he masks his tragedy, and at the beginning of chapter 15, his arrival into Lady Narborough's drawing room is preceded by the "large button-hole of Parma violets" bursting from his outfit. They're the flowers, of course, rather than the sweets named after them—though we think the latter are appropriately fancy.

Our recipe yields a gloriously deep-purple batch of the sweets: heady, floral, and impeccably well turned out.

Makes around 36 sweets

INGREDIENTS

3 tablespoons water, hot

2 drops violet food coloring, or a tiny dab, if using gel

¼ teaspoon violet flavor

1 teaspoon glucose (or corn syrup)

1½ teaspoons powdered gelatin

2 cups (250 grams) powdered sugar, sieved, plus extra for dusting

METHOD

1. Place the water in a small bowl and add the food coloring, flavor, and glucose (or corn syrup). Whisk until well combined. Add the gelatin and mix again.

2. Add the powdered sugar a couple of spoonfuls at a time and beat with a wooden spoon until mixed. Stop adding the sugar once the dough is stiff (you can add a little more if needed).

3. Dust a clean surface with powdered sugar and turn out the dough. Knead it until smooth—this should take around 5 minutes.

4. Divide the dough into eight pieces, working with one piece at a time and covering the rest with plastic wrap so it doesn't dry out. On your dusted surface, roll each piece into a skinny sausage—the diameter you'd like the sweets to be. Cut along the length in 2-millimeter slices.

5. Alternatively, roll each portion of dough to a thickness of around 2 millimeters and use a small cutter to shape your sweets.

6. Once you've used up all the dough, line a tray or board with parchment paper. Arrange the sweets in a single layer and set them aside to dry out. This should take around 12 hours, or until they're stiff.

Jambon Chaud-Froid

Cold and hot. Night and day. The turmoil and the peace. The portrait and the man. This is a novel packed with paradoxes and contradictions, and this dish—"untouched" by Dorian at a dinner party—sums it all up.

With layers of jellied sauce, typically a velouté thickened with gelatin, poured over a cooked ham, it has a sort of nightmarish beauty similar to dishes set in aspic. It won't preserve the ham or imbue it with eternal youth, but it will smooth over the edges as it encases a meaty center in a silken sauce.

The dish is perfect as a centerpiece at a dinner party or fancy buffet, and its sauce can also be made as a velvety cape for cold roast chicken or chicken breast fillets, a whole baked salmon, or a vegetarian alternative like roasted spiced cauliflower, coated in the sauce before being sprinkled with pomegranate seeds to serve.

Serves 4

INGREDIENTS

17½ ounces (500 grams) ham joint
2 ¾ tablespoons (40 grams) butter
⅓ cup (50 grams) all-purpose flour
1½ cups (350 milliliters) vegetable stock
2 teaspoons powdered gelatin
Chives, peppercorns, and edible flowers, to decorate

METHOD

1. Preheat the oven to 390°F/200°C/180°C fan/gas mark 6. Place the ham in a baking pan and cook it for around 35 minutes, or until cooked through. Line a baking pan and set the cooked ham aside on a wire rack in the pan (to catch any drips of sauce later).

2. Meanwhile, make a roux: melt the butter in a medium saucepan over medium heat and add the flour, stirring until it's well combined. Allow it to sizzle for another minute, then slowly add the stock, stirring as you go (use a whisk if it starts to look lumpy).

3. Bring it to a simmer, then remove the pan from the heat and whisk in the gelatin.

4. Pour a layer of the sauce evenly over the top and sides of the ham (aim to use between a quarter and a third of the sauce), then put it in the fridge for around 10 minutes to set.

5. Gently reheat the sauce, whisking again so it's silky, and pour over another layer, then return the ham to the fridge for another 10 minutes. Repeat once or twice more, so the sauce is mostly used up.

6. You can keep the ham in the fridge for up to 24 hours. When you're ready to serve, transfer it to a serving platter and decorate it with chives, peppercorns, and (if you want to be really fancy) edible flowers.

5

Best Served Bloody: Cold-Comfort Meals in Bram Stoker's *Dracula*

FOOD PROVIDES STRANGE COMFORT AND THOUGHTS OF HOME IN THE 1897 CLASSIC—UNTIL IT BECOMES A WEAPON AGAINST THE COUNT'S SEEMINGLY INSATIABLE APPETITE.

IT STARTS WITH warm thoughts of home and a bowl of chicken stew. Specifically, a serving of spicy, velvety paprika *hendl* or chicken *paprikash*, a traditional Hungarian stew laced with paprika. The deceptively simple supper makes such an impression on a fresh-off-the-train Jonathan Harker, dining alone at the Hotel Royale in Budapest, that he jots down a memo to "get recipe for Mina." His fiancée can, he imagines, re-create the "dinner, or rather supper, a chicken done up some way with red pepper."

When a novel is so familiar, and so ingrained in fictional fabric, as Bram Stoker's *Dracula*, it's hard to imagine reading those words without a fog of foreboding and a pang of pity. We know it doesn't work out so well for Jonathan and Mina. We know that the journal will soon take a much darker turn. And we can be pretty sure that Mina will never stand in front of a stove, Jonathan's journal propped open, following the scribbled recipe for a cozy supper for two.

There's a poignancy in Jonathan's simple observations and innocent memos. The dish to him is unfamiliar, exotic even, in a way that appeals to him but also makes him yearn for home and domesticity.

Like Count Dracula—whom Jonathan has, so far, only corresponded with—the dish feels strange, Other, and deliciously appealing. Jonathan is drawn to it in spite of, or perhaps because of, its difference. Yet he muffles the sense of danger by framing it within a familiar, human context.

As readers, we can almost taste that chicken paprikash, despite the perfunctory description. It's very good, Jonathan says, "but thirsty"—a simple review that evokes the pepperiness, the spiciness, and the velvety richness of the stew.

That night, Jonathan suffers "all sorts of queer dreams." A dog stands guard beneath his hotel room window, howling through the night. Perhaps, the hapless solicitor wonders, it "may have been the paprika." Yet he still devours more of the spice at breakfast, eating "a sort of porridge of maize flour" and "egg-plant stuffed with forcemeat." He adores these paprika-laced dishes so much that he adds another memo to get the recipes for Mina.

Jonathan is aware of the warning signs; he even jots them down in his journal. Still, he continues on his journey, shuffling toward danger as if he has no choice—or perhaps because he has a craving, or an appetite, for an excitement he can't quite name.

In the meantime, his journal focuses heavily on the minutiae, dominated by a bite-by-bite rundown of what he eats. One of the dishes he describes is "robber steak," which he explains is "bits of bacon, onion, and beef, seasoned with red pepper, and strung on sticks, and roasted over the fire, in simple style of the London cat's meat!" This is Jonathan's last supper before leaving for the castle in Transylvania, and the image of impalement and roasted flesh feels rather portentous. The food is becoming more sinister as the distance between Jonathan and the count shortens.

The links between Dracula and food run deep. On the most obvious level, Dracula—and other vampires of lore—feeds and survives by draining others' lifeblood. It's their means of sustenance and survival, the main (or at least most tangible) reason they terrify us, and, at least in the case of Count Dracula, their pleasure. It's sinful and hedonistic; it's pure greed and gluttony.

The vampire is hungry, and human blood is what he craves. In his *Dissertations sur les apparitions des anges* (1746), French Benedictine monk and "vampirologist" Dom Augustin Calmet muses that "the vampire has a sort of hunger" that drives him to eat his way out of his coffin and devour his every surviving relative. The only way to stop the ghost's reign of terror is by decapitating or "opening the heart" of the corpse. Then, consumption is again key, as he goes on to suggest mixing the blood with flour "to make bread of."

Gluttonous vampires predate Stoker's novel too. In the *Philosophical Dictionary* (1764) Voltaire describes vampires as "sucking corpses" who "grew fat, got rosy, and enjoyed an excellent appetite" as "the persons so sucked waned, grew pale, and fell into consumption." For Voltaire, however, it's the "true suckers"—the businessmen, bankers, and brokers—who live in "very agreeable palaces." Perhaps, as a literal bloodsucker and would-be property magnate, Count Dracula is an embodiment of both.

The count's appetite and his inability to control it are equated with excessive consumption, the uncivilized antithesis to mannered mealtimes. Initially, though, the very opposite raises suspicions and marks this shadowy character out as a little different: Dracula is odd in his abstinence of food. After eating several meals alone at the castle, Jonathan notes: "It is strange that as yet I have not seen the Count eat or drink. He must be a very peculiar man!"

As the story develops, and Jonathan's sense of dread looms larger, the descriptions of food become less vivid and detailed. They still feature, though. There's a welcome supper of cold roast chicken, cheese, and salad, the cloche removed from the dish by the count (who declares he does not "sup"). Breakfast is a spread of cold items. And they become starker and less appealing as time ticks by, perhaps because Jonathan no longer finds comfort in mealtime rituals—perhaps, also, because sustenance feels so at odds with his unsettling host and strange setting.

Eventually, Jonathan's appetite dissipates completely. Food is necessary purely for survival, not pleasure. And it becomes a weapon: the characters consume in order not to be consumed by the bloodthirsty count.

When the men undergo blood transfusions in the hope they can purge the vampire from bitten Lucy's body, Van Helsing's advice is to "lie on your sofa, and rest awhile, then have much breakfast and come here to me." Dr. Seward asks Mina to eat to better help her cope with her grief, suggesting that dinner will keep her strong for the "cruel and dreadful task" that lies before them.

Food becomes both a mark of difference between the human characters and Count Dracula's Other and a means of destroying the threat that the vampire represents.

It stands in stark contrast to the start of the novel, when a simple supper provided comfort and warm thoughts of home.

Mina's Paprika Hendl

Unlike Dracula's cold cuts, this traditional Hungarian dish—also known as paprikash—is a warm welcome in a bowl: thick, rich, and shot through with the subtle smokiness of paprika.

Serve the pink-sauced stew spooned over ribbons of black tagliatelle—usually colored by squid ink or activated charcoal—for full Gothic effect. It'll taste just as lovely accompanied by any pasta, potatoes, or rice, though. Or simply devour it with a spoon, perhaps with some chunky bread to mop up the sauce.

Serves 2 to 3

INGREDIENTS

2 tablespoons olive oil
17½ ounces (500 grams) boneless, skinless chicken thighs, cut into strips
2 tablespoons (30 grams) butter
1 onion, finely sliced
1 red pepper, finely sliced
1 clove garlic, finely chopped or minced
3 tablespoons smoked paprika
1 teaspoon hot paprika
Pinch of salt
1⅔ cups (400 grams) canned tomatoes, chopped
1½ cups (350 milliliters) chicken or vegetable stock
⅔ cups (150 milliliters) sour cream
Black tagliatelle, to serve (optional)

METHOD

1. Place the olive oil in a large heavy-bottomed saucepan or stewpot and, once hot, add the chicken, cooking over medium heat for 4 to 5 minutes on each side to brown. Remove and set aside.

2. Using the same pan, reduce the heat to low and add the butter. Once melted, add the onion and red pepper, cooking gently for 3 to 4 minutes, until soft.

3. Add the garlic, paprikas, and salt and cook for a further minute, taking care not to let the garlic brown.

4. Return the chicken to the pan, add the tomatoes, and simmer for a few minutes before adding the stock. Bring the mixture back to a simmer, cover, and cook on low to medium heat for around half an hour, removing the lid for the final 10 minutes or so to help the sauce reduce and thicken.

5. Add the sour cream, stirring gently. Continue cooking until heated through and serve over pasta or with your chosen accompaniment.

Make it vegetarian: Preheat the oven to 390°F/200°C/180°C fan/gas mark 6. Dice the flesh of half a butternut squash, add it to an ovenproof dish, drizzle with 1 tablespoon olive oil, and season with a little salt, then roast for 20 minutes. Give the dish a shake, add 7 ounces (200 grams) sliced mushrooms, then roast for a further 20 minutes. Follow the recipe from step 2, adding the oil along with the butter, and throw the roasted veg into the pan in place of the chicken at step 4, simmering for just 15 to 20 minutes, until the sauce is nicely reduced.

Impletata with Forcemeat

A NIGHT DISTURBED BY queer dreams, a dog howling outside the hotel window, and (Jonathan imagines) too-spicy food doesn't put our narrator off his breakfast—even though that involves "more paprika." Alongside a polenta dish, *mămăligă*, Jonathan tucks into "egg-plant stuffed with forcemeat," apparently named *impletata.*

There doesn't seem to be an actual eggplant dish that fits the description, though forcemeat refers to finely ground, seasoned meat, such as that used for sausages. This recipe works with sausage meat or any ground meat (such as pork or beef) and can easily be made vegan with plant-based meat, finely chopped mushrooms, or lentils.

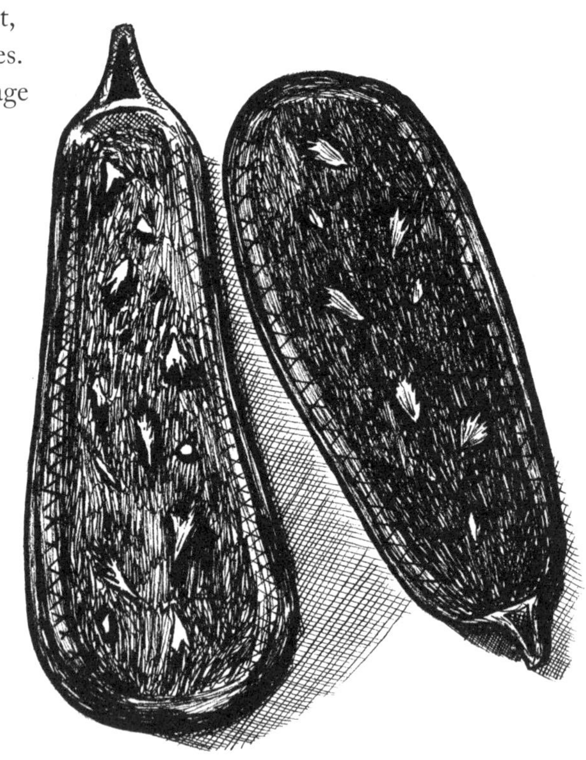

Serve with peppery greens as a light meal or starter or with a wedge of our Cheesy Baked Mămăligă (page 64).

Serves 4

INGREDIENTS

2 medium eggplants
2 cloves garlic
2 tablespoons olive oil, divided
Salt and freshly ground black pepper

SAUCE

½ onion, finely chopped
7 ounces (200 grams) sausage meat or ground beef
1⅔ cups (400 grams) canned diced tomatoes
4 tablespoons harissa paste
Salt and finely ground black pepper
Handful of finely chopped flat-leaf parsley, to garnish

METHOD

1. Preheat the oven to 390°F/200°C/180°C fan/gas mark 6. Halve the eggplants lengthwise and, using a small, sharp knife, score a criss-cross pattern into the flesh, stopping around 1 centimeter from the skin (and taking care not to pierce through).

2. Slice the garlic lengthwise to create medium-fine shards, then gently press them into the cut parts of the eggplants, distributing evenly between the halves.

3. Drizzle each half with 1 tablespoon of the oil, season with salt and pepper, and press the eggplant halves back together. Wrap each one in foil, arrange them on a baking sheet, and place in the oven for around 45 minutes, or until the flesh is soft and tender. Remove the vegetables from the oven and set them aside, still in the foil, to cool slightly.

4. Meanwhile, to make the sauce, add the remaining 1 tablespoon olive oil to a casserole dish and, over low to medium heat, gently fry the onion until soft.

5. Add the ground beef or sausage meat and continue to cook, stirring regularly, until nicely browned and cooked through.

6. Stir in the tomatoes and add the harissa paste, adding a splash of water if it looks quite thick.

7. Season to taste with salt and pepper and continue to simmer for a further 15 minutes, stirring occasionally.

8. Meanwhile, once the eggplants are cool enough to handle, use two spoons to gently scoop out most of the flesh, taking care not to break the skin (it's easier if they're still warm). Transfer the flesh to a board and roughly chop it before adding it to the sauce.

9. Arrange the eggplant shells in an ovenproof dish and spoon in the sauce. If you have extra, you can either overstuff them so the sauce overflows into the dish, or set the sauce aside and warm it up before serving it on the side. (You could also keep it as a sauce for pasta.)

10. Place the eggplants back into the oven to warm through (around 10 minutes), then sprinkle with parsley to serve.

Cheesy Baked Mămăligă

The other element of Jonathan's Transylvanian breakfast is mămăligă, which he describes as "a sort of porridge of maize flour." It's actually polenta. In Romania, mămăligă is a staple that's served with many meals, typically in a sturdy, sliceable style and with a dollop of sour cream.

For this recipe, it's topped with cheese and crisped up in the oven for the perfect accompaniment to our stuffed eggplants (or impletata), especially with any extra sauce spooned on top. Any leftovers are lovely with salad, topped with stew, or just eaten cold, in squares.

Serves 4 to 6

INGREDIENTS

4¼ cups (1 liter) water
1½ cups (250 grams) polenta
½ cup (50 grams) cheddar, cut into small cubes
2 teaspoons chili flakes

Salt and freshly ground black pepper

2 tablespoons of butter

2¼ tablespoons (25 grams) Parmesan, finely grated

Sour cream, to serve

METHOD

1. Preheat the oven to 390°F/200°C/180°C fan/gas mark 6. Place the water in a large saucepan and bring it to a boil. Reduce the heat to a simmer, then slowly add the polenta, whisking as you go.

2. Switch to a wooden spoon (the mixture will quickly become too stiff for a whisk) and continue to stir for 10 to 15 minutes, until the polenta is thick and comes away from the sides of the pan easily.

3. Remove from the heat and stir in the cheddar and chili flakes. Season well with salt and pepper.

4. Use the butter to grease a 9-inch (23-centimeter) square oven dish. Transfer the polenta into the dish and use a spatula to distribute it evenly.

5. Sprinkle the polenta with Parmesan and bake it in the oven for 10 to 15 minutes, until the cheese is golden and slightly crispy. Cut it into squares and serve with a dollop of sour cream.

Robber Steak

Jonathan's last supper before setting off on his fateful journey to meet Count Dracula could hardly sound less appetizing. He dines on "robber steak," made up of "bits of bacon, onion, and beef" strung on sticks. It's a meal he likens to "the London cat's meat."

It doesn't sound like something one would necessarily rush to re-create in a home kitchen, though he was referring to meat *for* cats: scraps of horsemeat and other by-products sold cheaply to pet owners.

OK, still not particularly appetizing. But our version, made with steak, fat chunks of pancetta, peppers, and onions, is delicious—and sure to be a hit at barbecues, charred over glowing coals.

For a vegan version, replace the meat with chunks of firm tofu or sliced vegetarian sausages and either omit the bacon or use a substitute.

Serves 2 to 3 (6 skewers)

INGREDIENTS

2 red peppers, whole

10½ ounces (300 grams) sirloin steak, cut into large chunks

2 tablespoons olive oil

2 tablespoons paprika

6 shallots, peeled and halved

10½ ounces (300 grams) pancetta, cubed

METHOD

1. If using wooden skewers, submerge them in water for at least 10 minutes before using—this helps to ensure that they won't catch or burn while cooking.

2. To remove the skin from the peppers, flash-cook them over a gas burner or stove flame, on a hot barbecue, or under a very hot grill, until the skin begins to blister and blacken in places. Allow the peppers to cool before rubbing the skin off and cutting them into generous chunks.

3. In large bowl toss the beef chunks with the olive oil and paprika until well covered.

4. Begin assembling the skewers, threading on the peppers, beef, shallots, and pancetta as you wish. Take care not to pack them too tightly, as this prevents even cooking.

5. Place them directly on the hot barbecue, or in a griddle or large frying pan over medium heat, and cook for 15 to 20 minutes, turning occasionally, until the beef is sizzling and browned and the pancetta cubes are cooked through and nicely crisp.

Florence Balcombe's Dracula Salad

IF SALAD SEEMS an unlikely inclusion among recipes inspired by *Dracula*, the image of Bram Stoker vacationing by the seaside is even more incongruous.

He and his wife, Florence Balcombe, made regular trips to Port Erroll (now Cruden Bay), a fishing village on Scotland's northeast coast. The author wrote there, and shortly after his death, so did his widow. In 1912, she contributed this, along with a meatier recipe for fried plums rolled in bacon, to a church pamphlet called *Cruden Recipes and Wrinkles.*

"Arrange alternate slices of ripe tomatoes, and ripe, purple, egg-shaped plums in dish, and dress with oil and vinegar French dressing," she wrote.

We've taken her short and sweet idea as the inspiration for this juicy salad packed with beet, blood orange, and tomatoes. Eat it for a simple lunch or supper with fresh, crusty bread or serve as a suitably dark and mysterious salad at your next Gothic dinner party.

Serves 2 as a main or 4 as a starter or side dish

INGREDIENTS

2 cups (300 grams) raw or precooked beets
1 blood orange, peel and pith removed, sliced
5 large ripe tomatoes, sliced
4–5 small ripe plums, sliced
½ cup (100 grams) feta
1 tablespoon finely chopped fresh mint
1 tablespoon finely chopped fresh thyme
1 tablespoon finely chopped fresh flat-leaf parsley
1 tablespoon roughly chopped walnuts
Pinch of chili flakes, to serve (optional)

Dressing

Juice of ½ lime
1 tablespoon red wine vinegar
2 tablespoons olive oil
Salt and freshly ground black pepper

METHOD

1. If using fresh beets, preheat the oven to 390°F/200°C/180°C fan/gas mark 6. Scrub the beets to remove any dirt. Place them on a baking sheet and roast them for 30 to 40 minutes, until tender. You should be able to pierce them with a skewer or sharp knife with little resistance. Set them aside to cool completely.

2. Peel the cooled beets (or if using precooked, drain off any liquid) and slice them to roughly the same thickness as the orange, plums, and tomatoes. Layer everything up in a large, shallow dish or on a serving plate.

3. To make the dressing, in a small bowl whisk together the lime juice, red wine vinegar, olive oil, a little salt, and a crack of black pepper.

4. Just before serving, drizzle over the dressing, crumble over the feta, and sprinkle on the chopped herbs, walnuts, and chili flakes, if using.

6

The Tyranny of Tea, and Tales Told by Tangerines, in Daphne du Maurier's *Rebecca*

IN THIS 1938 MASTERPIECE, NOTHING IS QUITE AS IT SEEMS—NOT EVEN THE SANDWICHES.

IT'S HALF PAST four at Manderley: time for tea. There's no need to ring the bell, madam. Mrs. Danvers keeps a punctual household. There is Frith, the butler, neatly folded at the waist as he smooths imaginary creases and brushes away nonexistent crumbs from the crisp, snow-white tablecloth. There's Robert, the footman, whom Frith instructs with an arch of the eyebrow, a flicker of a gloved hand.

The "stately little performance" proceeds with the placement of platters of crumpets (dripping with butter), crisp wedges of toast, and floury scones. A catwalk of cakes (three kinds!) totters behind. Tea is poured from a "monstrous" silver teapot, kept topped up with water from the matching spirit kettle with its little flame.

Daphne du Maurier wasn't one to waste words. Unlike the glorious yet grotesquely wasteful afternoon teas served daily in the coastal mansion, every crumb, every daub of icing, every drip of butter is designed to be devoured. Her deliciously detailed descriptions of food make us, as readers, hungry, yet they do so much more. In *Rebecca*, du Maurier's food writing hints that Something Else Is Going On. It denotes social status (and social awkwardness), sounds a warning, portends doom, and reveals, in its shadows, the glimmer of a ghost.

Right from the first few pages, food fuels the storytelling. The second Mrs. de Winter describes the "little ritual" of their tea, which she and husband,

Maxim, take daily in their little hotel: two slices of buttered bread and cups of China tea. Their new life, though hardly one of hardship, is distinctly different and stripped of status, and nowhere is the comparison starker than in the juxtaposition of this with the lavish afternoon teas of Manderley.

The dining habits of the never-named narrator chart her social standing throughout the novel. Her journey to Manderley begins in Monte Carlo, where she is staying as a companion to Mrs. Van Hopper—a wealthy American woman depicted as vulgar to the point of grotesqueness and a marvelous (if fleeting) Gothic creation.

The narrator gnaws miserably on comfortless, chewy, badly carved cold cuts, sent back to the kitchen by a dissatisfied customer and thrust upon her by a waiter who "sensed [her] position as inferior." Mrs. Van Hopper, meanwhile, gleefully gobbles on fresh ravioli, clutching her fork in "fat, bejeweled fingers," and dribbling sauce down her chin.

Cold cuts and insulting leftovers are among the novel's recurring food themes, intertwining with a battle for control of the kitchen and menus decided on the whims of a ghost.

Even before stepping through the door and into her new life at Manderley, the narrator has a longing for the warm domesticity of her imaginings. They whoosh by cottages as she fancies herself in her "kitchen, clean as a pin, laying the table for supper." This tale is told with hindsight, of course, so we can't really know whether she had such fantasies on the road to Manderley. It's likely, though, that her misgivings truly began after getting acquainted with Mrs. Danvers: an "extraordinary woman," as Maxim puts it. Mildly.

The kitchens at Manderley do not belong to our narrator. They belong to a ghost; they belong to Rebecca. Mrs. Danvers controls every cake, every crumpet, every cup of tea that makes its way, with stiff formality, to the drawing room, and she surveys every soufflé that makes its way to the dinner table. She is there to serve Mrs. de Winter and does this by making sure everything, from scrambled eggs to sauces, is made according to her wishes.

The problem, for our narrator, is that it's *another* Mrs. de Winter she answers to. The housekeeper uses food to demonstrate how unworthy she deems the second Mrs. de Winter to be. She takes control of the menu planning, exposes Maxim's new bride with questions she knows she can't answer, and asks for opinions she suspects have not been formed. (Rebecca, meanwhile, "was most particular about her sauces.")

Food is a prison of someone else's making, trapping the narrator with its rituals and formality. She yearns to nibble on cucumber sandwiches under the chestnut tree; instead, she battles with a monstrous teapot and endures "the paraphernalia of a stiff tea." They eat the food that Rebecca liked, and that insidious presence shrinks the narrator. Her every move, from holding a pen to clutching a knife and fork, is haunted by this person who apparently did everything with a far greater degree of elegance, charm, and grace. She swerves decisions and allows the housekeeper to make them. She complains to Maxim that she sees herself as "like a between-maid": subservient, impermanent, insignificant.

Then comes the fateful ball. The buffet is a facsimile of those laid out at past balls, when Rebecca worked the room. Our narrator didn't have to "bother [her] head" about anything. Later, humiliated by her dress faux pas, she is haunted by a different woman, dressed in "a salmon-colored gown hooped in crinoline form." She sways in and out of view, smiling as if on cue. The narrator's description suggests the "salmon lady" is an extra in a vacuous, vaguely threatening theatrical performance.

Frozen, as if in fear of forgetting her role, during "God Save the King," this salmon lady then attacks a plate of chicken in aspic "in a sort of frenzy." Again, we readers are left to ponder how much of this springs from the narrator's fitful imagination. People, objects, and even plates of food become monstrous and menacing, as if conspiring against her.

When, later on in the novel, she does decide to wrest some control, it's via the kitchens. Back to those rejected cold cuts. Having previously balked at the thought of how much food is wasted and wondering whether "minions" are being fed with their leftovers, the second Mrs. de Winter is now incensed by the thought that they might be "still living on the remains" from the ball. Her first act of war is to insist on "something hot" and to do so behind Mrs. Danvers's back (which, predictably, does not go down well).

Maxim, meanwhile, is far too important to get involved in this cold (cuts) war. The "business of tea was a side-issue that did not matter to him," his new wife observes. The widower is portrayed as dark and dashing, though it could be argued that he is the real villain—and that it's food that gives him away. He plays host as his wife sweats behind a steaming kettle. He precedes an apology with an instruction to pour him a cup of tea and, later on, scolds her for talking with her mouth full (while telling her to "eat up [her] peaches").

Maxim's oppressive, controlling nature is highlighted when he's away, having his "man's dinner" in London. The narrator feels a "lightness of heart," a giddiness that reminds her of childhood. Having politely picked and miserably nibbled at most meals at Manderley, she now enjoys a stolen clutch of Bath Oliver cookies—six of them—and an apple. She chides herself for allowing the thought that this sense of freedom (and renewed appetite) could be because her husband is away. Mrs. Danvers makes a far more convenient villain.

Yet the signs were always there (or, perhaps, she now threads them into her narrative, subconsciously signposting the danger ahead).

Early on in their "romance," while still in Monte Carlo, Maxim's relatively modest in-room breakfast—"coffee, a boiled egg, toast, marmalade, and a tangerine"—rather gives the game away. He places his order, then begins to file his nails. It sets the scene for an equally unceremonious proposal—surely among the least romantic ever written—and makes clear that this is a mere formality for him. A business matter, and not a particularly important one, at that. But is there something more sinister here, a hint of darkness beneath the mannered yet rather brusque surface of the man?

Take the tangerine. Actually, don't: it's rather sour. Bitter, in fact. Still, let's look at it. Proposal/transaction taken care of, he offers his new fiancée a few segments of the fruit. They are sour. *Very* sour. They leave a "sharp, bitter taste" in her mouth. In case we missed it, du Maurier continues to pour acidity onto the page. The effect, as a reader, is visceral. We can feel the sourness to the point of puckering our lips; we can taste the bitter, pithy, "pale" segments. Maxim, the narrator worries, has not "said anything yet about being in love." He was in a hurry, perhaps, and it was breakfast. "Marmalade, and coffee, and that tangerine. No time. The tangerine was very bitter."

How different, and uneventful, her life could have been if she had only listened to her taste buds and heeded the warning of the tangerine.

Tea at Half Past Four

Manderley's daily afternoon tea is served with elegance and a frigid sort of fuss that contrasts with the crackle of the fire and the array of toasty, typically comforting baked goods being served. You might want to serve yours in a more relaxed manner or devour it with the type of abandon the second Mrs. de Winter reserves for some sneaky Bath Oliver cookies.

Use these recipes to re-create the entire afternoon tea spread or dip in and out for your own little slice of Manderley.

Those Dripping Crumpets

We can see them now . . . can't you? Inflating upward and bubbling away on the griddle, then flipped—at just the right moment—to gild their tops. This recipe, based on using one egg, makes a good batch of crumpets. If you're not inclined to eat the lot within a few days, they can be frozen and defrosted before toasting. Though we suspect you might not require this information, because homemade crumpets are a treat destined to be greedily devoured.

Makes 10 *to* 12 *crumpets*

INGREDIENTS

2⅓ cups (300 grams) all-purpose flour, sifted
4 teaspoons baking powder
½ teaspoon salt
1¾ tablespoons (25 grams) butter, melted
1 egg, beaten
2 cups (500 milliliters) milk, slightly warmed
Sunflower or rapeseed oil, for greasing

METHOD

1. Place the flour in a large bowl, add the baking powder and salt, and stir to combine.

2. Make a well in the middle and pour in the butter, stirring. Do the same with the egg and, finally, the milk, adding the latter slowly and stopping when the batter is the consistency of a thick custard or just-melted ice cream. (You might not need all of the milk.) Decant into a large jug.

3. Grease a griddle or a heavy-bottomed frying pan with a little oil and grease inside your crumpet rings too—just use however many you have (and what fits on your griddle or in your pan) to cook the crumpets in batches.

4. Heat the pan or griddle, with the crumpet rings, on medium-low, and pour batter into the rings so each is around a third full. They will rise up and begin to bubble.

5. Once they're bubbling well and the batter looks quite solid, carefully remove the rings (use tongs or potholders), giving them a wiggle if they're being stubborn. Quickly and carefully flip the crumpets with a spatula.

6. Wait a minute or so, then remove the crumpets from the heat and set them aside. Continue as above until all the batter is finished, greasing the griddle or pan and the crumpet rings between each batch.

7. To serve, toast the crumpets lightly on each side and smother them with butter, jam, or anything else you fancy.

Hot, Floury Scones

OUR PROTAGONIST RARELY actually *eats* any of the afternoon tea spreads laid out for her. Perhaps she realizes that every element—including the "piping hot and floury" scones—is prepared as Rebecca demanded. So, instead, she prefers to steal a few crumbs to nibble on when no one's looking.

Hopefully you'll feel free to eat these scones with gusto. Taking "hot" as a clue, this recipe yields scones meant to be split, buttered, and scoffed straight from the oven, though they will keep in an airtight container for a few days.

Makes around 12

INGREDIENTS

2 cups (250 grams) all-purpose flour

Pinch of salt

1 teaspoon baking powder

2 tablespoons (30 grams) butter, fridge cold and cubed, plus extra for greasing

1 egg

⅔ cup (150 milliliters) sour cream

METHOD

1. Preheat the oven to 430°F/220°C/200°C fan/gas mark 7. Grease a large baking sheet.

2. Sift the dry ingredients into a large bowl and rub the butter in with your fingertips to form the texture of coarse breadcrumbs.

3. In a small bowl beat together the egg and sour cream and add to the dry ingredients, mixing gradually to form a dough.

4. Flour a surface and turn out the dough. Knead it until smooth, then roll it out to a thickness of around 1½ centimeters.

5. Using a 5-centimeter cutter, cut out rounds and lay them on the baking sheet.

6. Bake for 10 to 15 minutes, until risen, lightly golden, and cooked through.

Sandwiches of an Unknown Nature

Du maurier's description of the sandwiches sounds suitably creepy, yet most of us have an inkling of what she means: those spreads and pastes that are simultaneously familiar and mysterious, usually involving cheese, fish, or egg and laced with lots of butter or mayonnaise. Around the time of *Rebecca*'s publication, cheese sandwiches—made with equal quantities of grated cheese and butter, mixed with a little cayenne pepper—were popular, as was this egg and shrimp filling.

Serves 2

INGREDIENTS

2 hard-boiled eggs, cooled and peeled, roughly chopped
1 cup (100 grams) cooked and peeled shrimp, roughly chopped
3½ tablespoons (50 grams) butter, melted, or 2 tablespoons mayonnaise
Pinch of cayenne pepper
Salt and freshly ground black pepper
4 medium slices bread

METHOD

1. Place the eggs and shrimp in a large bowl and stir in the butter.

2. Add the cayenne pepper and season to taste with salt and pepper and if using butter, allow the mixture to sit for a minute or two so it isn't runny.

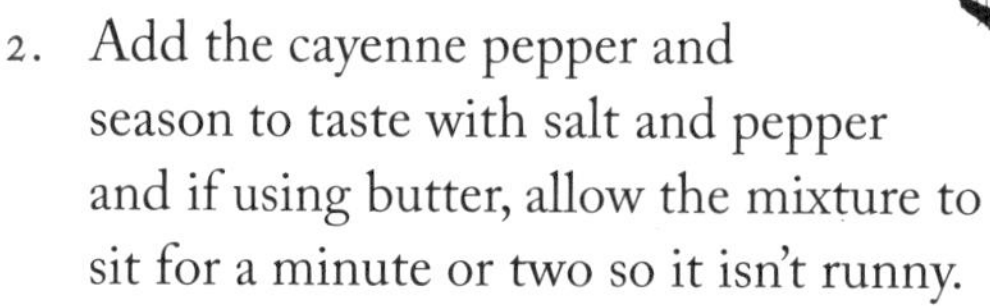

3. Spoon the mixture onto half of the bread slices, spread it out, then top with the other slices. Cut the sandwiches into dainty triangles that would make Mrs. Danvers proud. Maybe.

That Very Special Gingerbread

AMONG THE DISHES that make up the lavish spread is "that very special gingerbread." Du Maurier doesn't elaborate on what makes it so very special, so we've based ours on a classic Victorian loaf, brightened it with a brisk lemon icing, and enriched it with a glug of rum.

Serves 6 to 8

INGREDIENTS

½ cup (125 grams) unsalted butter
1⅓ cup (200 grams) soft brown sugar
⅔ cup (250 grams) black molasses
3¼ cups (400 grams) all-purpose flour
1 teaspoon baking soda
1 tablespoon ground ginger
2 eggs, beaten
3 tablespoons rum, or 1 teaspoon rum flavoring or lemon extract
Zest of ½ lemon

Lemon Glaze

½ cup (50 grams) powdered sugar
Juice of ½ lemon (plus a little more if needed)
Zest of 1 lemon

METHOD

1. Preheat the oven to 350°F/180°C/160°C fan/gas mark 4. Butter a standard loaf pan (around 8.5 by 4.5 inches or 24 by 12 centimeters) and line it with parchment paper.

2. Place the butter, brown sugar, and molasses in a small saucepan and melt over low heat, stirring for around 5 minutes, or until the sugar has dissolved and the mixture is smooth.

3. Sieve the flour, baking soda, and ginger into a large mixing bowl. Make a well in the middle and beat in the eggs.

4. Add the mixture from the saucepan along with the rum and lemon zest. Beat, using a wooden spoon, until combined.

5. Pour into the prepared pan and bake for 45 minutes, then test with a wooden skewer. If, when inserted into the center, the skewer comes out almost clean (you still want a little stickiness), the gingerbread is done. Otherwise, pop it back in for another 5 to 10 minutes, covering loosely with foil if it's browning too quickly.

6. Leave the loaf in the pan until cool enough to touch, then tip it onto a wire rack to cool completely.

7. To make the glaze, sieve the powdered sugar into a small bowl and gradually add the lemon juice until you have a smooth, slightly runny icing, adding more juice if needed.

8. Once the loaf has cooled completely, drizzle over the icing and scatter the zest over the top. Allow it to set before slicing to serve.

Angel Cake, That Melted in the Mouth

THERE ARE SEVERAL variations of angel cake, though the description strongly suggests that the one served at Manderley was a take on the angel food cake—light as air and with the texture of marshmallow—popular in the US and brought to British kitchens via women's magazines and cookbooks.

Serves 8 *to* 10

INGREDIENTS

⅔ cup (75 grams) all-purpose flour
¾ cup (150 grams) superfine sugar
10 egg whites
1 teaspoon cream of tartar
¾ teaspoon vanilla extract

METHOD

1. Preheat the oven to 320°F/160°C/140°C fan/gas mark 3. Place the flour and sugar in one small bowl and sift it several times between another bowl, until superfine.

2. In a large bowl whisk the egg whites with the cream of tartar to form stiff peaks. Continue whisking while gradually adding half of the sugar and flour mixture.

3. Beat for a minute or so, then beat in the vanilla before gently folding in the rest of the sugar and flour mixture until well combined and silky.

4. Pour or spoon into a deep 8-inch (20-centimeter) round cake pan (not greased or lined and without a loose bottom) and bake for 40 to 45 minutes, increasing the temperature to 375°F/190°C/170°C fan/gas mark 5 for the final 10 to 15 minutes. It should be a light golden color and feel springy to the touch. Cover loosely with foil if it starts to brown too quickly.

5. Remove the pan from the oven and invert it over a large plate or wooden board (this prevents the cake from sinking as it cools).

6. Allow the cake to cool. It may wiggle its way down to the plate. If not, use a spatula to fully release it from the pan. Flip it onto another plate or cake stand to serve.

The Rather Stodgier Cousin

THIS CLASSIC POUND cake, "bursting with peel and raisins," might be hearty and thick, but it's also more delectable, deliciously rich with butter and dried fruit.

Serves 10 *to* 12

INGREDIENTS

1 cup (250 grams) butter, softened
1⅓ cup (250 grams) superfine sugar
4 eggs
2 cups (250 grams) all-purpose flour
½ teaspoon baking powder
2⅓ cups (350 grams) currants, mixed peel, and sultanas (roughly equal quantities)
½ cup (50 grams) sliced almonds, crumbled
Zest of 2 lemons
3 tablespoons brandy (optional)
Powdered sugar, for dusting

METHOD

1. Preheat the oven to 320°F/160°C/140°C fan/gas mark 3. Grease and line a deep 8-inch (20-centimeter) round cake pan.

2. Cream together the butter and sugar, using a handheld whisk or stand mixer, until pale and fluffy. Add the eggs and mix, one at a time, until well incorporated.

3. In a medium bowl sift together the flour and baking powder and add, slowly, to the mix before stirring in the fruit, almonds, lemon zest, and brandy, if using.

4. Scrape the batter into the prepared cake pan and bake for around 2 hours, or until it's a deep golden brown and a wooden skewer inserted into the center comes out clean. Cover loosely with foil if it threatens to burn.

5. Cool the cake, still in the pan, on a wire rack before turning it out onto a plate or fancy cake stand. Dust with a little powdered sugar.

NEW YORK CAF
WE ARE
OPEN

7
Hungry Hearts and Seeking Solace in Sundaes in Carson McCullers's *The Heart Is a Lonely Hunter*

DISPARATE CHARACTERS ARE DESPERATELY SEEKING SUSTENANCE OF A DEEPER KIND IN THIS PRICKLY, AND AT TIMES TERRIBLY SAD, EXAMPLE OF SOUTHERN GOTHIC.

THERE ARE MOMENTS when *The Heart Is a Lonely Hunter* feels like a postapocalyptic zombie novel. Characters pound the pavements with pinched, pained expressions, their collars turned against the cold winds. When summer brings its burning heat, they wander in a hazy daze, sweaty and shuffling, ambling and aimless. Often, their faces wear "the desperate look of hunger and of loneliness."

No one is out hunting humans, however—at least not in a flesh-eating sense. They're hunting hearts. Some, like John Singer, are seeking something they fear is lost forever, while others scour the streets for something they've never had and can't quite name.

Carson McCullers's novel, which made its young author an overnight success when it was published in 1940, is a fine example of Southern Gothic. This subgenre employs many of the usual Gothic devices, weaving in hints of darkness, shadows of malice, and an unshakeable uneasiness that something bad is about to happen. It takes all of these elements and transports them to the American South, where temperatures can be bitingly cold or simmering hot and threatening to boil over. McCullers's characters, rubbing along uncomfortably in a small Georgia town during the Great Depression, behave in a similar way.

Much of the narrative centers around Singer, who, deaf and mute, is silent on the surface yet haunted by loud thoughts and bittersweet memories. Others flock to Singer and imagine that he, more than anyone else, understands them.

One is Mick Kelly, a strong-willed young girl with dreams too big for this mill town. "Mister Singer" boards at Mick's family home, and she finds some semblance of peace in his presence. So do others, including the well-meaning but dangerously self-destructive Jake Blount, who arrives in town with plans to fight social injustice and racism but too often falls to drink in his disillusionment.

Biff Brannon, owner of the New York Café and observer of his customers' lives (though this borders on an uncomfortable obsession with Mick), is also drawn to Singer's "many-tinted gentle eyes" that are "grave as a sorcerer's." And for Doctor Benedict Copeland, Singer seems to be the only person who understands his intellectual theories and the profound inequalities he faces as a Black doctor in a segregated town.

They visit at every opportunity, convinced "that the mute would always understand whatever they wanted to say to him. And maybe even more than that." He sates their hunger to be seen and understood and sometimes feeds them in a literal sense, too, from a tin box with bread, oranges, and cheese (he eats little himself).

Each one projects their hopes onto Singer, using him as a sounding board for their worries and fears, and he never disappoints. How can he, when they never really see him or hear his thoughts? Yet he might just be the loneliest of all. The one he loved, with whom he shared a real connection, has been taken away from him.

The novel opens with this ill-fated love story, of how Singer and his companion, Spiros Antonapoulos, are torn apart. Antonapoulos, sometimes referred to in the novel as "the Greek," is to Singer what Singer becomes to everyone else in the town: the one person who, he feels, understands him and touches his soul. They live together, take meals together, and walk "arm in arm" together to work. Before they depart, Singer leaves Antonapoulos with a hand on his arm and a lingering gaze, which is nothing if not a way of communicating love.

Antonapoulos's biggest love, though, is food. He works in his cousin's fruit store, making sweets and desserts. At home, he cooks their meals slowly, savoring every mouthful when he eats.

Later, separated from his friend and with only his hungry visitors for company, Singer takes his meals alone at the New York Café. People crowd him with their needs and demands, most of which he can't comprehend, and he feels overwhelmed. His mind is already fully occupied with memories of Antonapoulos, of his face "round and oily, with a wise and gentle smile."

Food is intertwined with those memories. He remembers his friend making a batch of caramel fudge, describing how it lay "golden and glossy" on the marble-topped table and how the air was sweetly scented with its buttered aroma. Antonapoulos is happy in his work and enjoys being observed. He also enjoys feeding others and making them laugh (to this end, he plunges his wet hand into a boiling vat of syrup).

Singer isn't so spontaneous, eating his meals quietly and thoughtfully and providing food for others with a formality that borders on the ceremonious. This is perhaps one of the reasons he so deeply admires Antonapoulos—the way he eats life up with gleeful abandon, nevertheless savoring every morsel and crumb.

Toward the end of the novel, his visit to his friend is impeccably planned, right down to the gifts: a deluxe basket of fruit, wrapped in cellophane, and a crate of perfectly ripe strawberries. Having arrived at his hotel after a train journey, and killing time before he can see Antonapoulos, Singer orders a room service breakfast of "broiled bluefish, hominy, French toast, and hot black coffee," then gets dressed as if for a wedding, before heading to his long-awaited reunion.

Later, he dwells on those strawberries, described as "large as walnuts," at the peak of ripeness and topped with tiny green bouquets. Yet the "subtle flavor of decay" is already creeping in. Singer, broken by recent news, continues to eat "until his palate is dulled by the taste." It's a significant moment. Food was both Antonapoulos's love and his way of communicating love to others. Through this, he transferred a sense of enjoyment of life to Singer. With that taken away, nothing tastes the same. His meals have become solitary and joyless.

Mick, too, reveals her loneliness through food. Dissatisfied with her life and lacking any meaningful connection to anyone except (she feels) Singer, she drifts into a fantasy of stealing "wintergreen candy" from the New York Café. She compares emotional emptiness to hunger, with the latter being preferable: "The feeling was a whole lot worse than being hungry for any dinner, yet it was like that." She wants *something*—but what?

Growing up in a poor family, Mick is used to being hungry. As her dreams of being a concert pianist slip away and disillusionment takes over, even a plate piled with meat, gravy, and grits can't fill her up.

Toward the end of the novel, a grief-stricken Mick seeks solace in the New York Café and ice cream. Now working (at Woolworth's), she has a little money to buy her own food. But she isn't keen on a sensible plate of roast chicken or veal stew, as suggested by Biff (who also invites her to have supper with him). No—she wants "a chocolate sundae and a nickel glass of draw beer." Beer was Singer's daily tipple, and the ice cream accompaniment suggests someone stuck between worlds—of childhood and adulthood and of this town and somewhere else. Mick doesn't really belong anywhere, and that's perhaps the one thing that connects McCullers's characters. (There's an extra layer of tragedy, then, that they are unable to reach each other.)

Food is shown, at times, to be a comfort, from Mick's love of hot chocolate to meals shared by the town's "two mutes." Other times, and for the most part, it evokes bittersweet memories that it cannot quite heal—and even the most satisfying meal (or bowl of ice cream) isn't enough to meet the raw edges of grief and loneliness.

Bourbon and Caramel Fudge

John Singer's memories of his beloved Spiros Antonapoulos often feature food, and the description of the latter making "a batch of caramel fudge" in the back room of his cousin's store is particularly luscious.

This recipe is made with condensed milk and laced with bourbon or whiskey (you could also use rum or a flavored liqueur, replace with essence, or omit altogether). A sprinkle of sea salt on top, before it sets, emphasizes and cuts through the rich caramel flavor.

Makes 30 to 36 squares

INGREDIENTS

1 (14-ounce or 400-gram) can condensed milk

⅔ cup (150 milliliters) whole milk

2 cups (400 grams) soft dark brown sugar

1 stick (120 grams) butter

1 teaspoon vanilla extract or paste

3 tablespoons bourbon or whiskey, or 1 teaspoon flavoring

Flaky sea salt

METHOD

1. Grease and line an 8-inch (20-centimeter) square pan. Place the condensed milk, milk, sugar, and butter in a medium saucepan over low heat, stirring until the sugar dissolves.

2. Raise the heat to medium-high and bring to a rapid boil. Allow the mixture to bubble for 10 to 15 minutes, stirring frequently, until it reaches a temperature of 240°F/115°C. (If you don't have a sugar thermometer, drop a small amount into a glass of cold water. If it forms a ball you can fish out, it's ready.)

3. Remove the pan from the heat and beat in the vanilla and bourbon, if using.

4. Pour the mixture into the prepared pan, allow it to cool for around 10 minutes, then sprinkle over a generous pinch of flaky sea salt.

5. Leave to set (around 2 to 3 hours) before cutting into squares.

Red Deviled Eggs

MICK KELLY HAS a habit of fixating on certain people, searching for that one person who will ease her loneliness. Of course, they don't really exist—the loneliness belongs to her and is hers to bear alone.

Before Singer, there was Celeste, a sixth-grader with long blonde hair, "a turned-up nose," and freckles. Mick never speaks to her, afraid she'll be rebuffed or perhaps disappointed by the reality of her imaginary new best friend.

Her memories of Celeste center around food: her blue tin lunchbox, the orange she ate at recess, and the "stuffed hard-boiled egg" she would hold and mash with her thumb. (Later, Harry does the same, reviving this vivid food memory.)

Perhaps if Mick had invited Celeste over for supper, they could have feasted on a slightly fancier take on those stuffed eggs: these deviled eggs, dyed a vibrant pinky-red with beetroot juice and filled with a spiced-up blend of the yolks and beetroot purée. Often known as salad or dressed eggs when served at church functions or funerals (to avoid the association with Satan), they're named deviled eggs because of their spicy nature.

The recipe can be fiddly, but it's worth the effort, especially for a party. A jar of pickled beetroot works best, as the juice is perfect for dyeing the eggs, though you could also use vacuum-packed beetroot and top up with a mix of beetroot juice and red wine vinegar (see steps 4 and 6). If you have any beetroot left over, chop it up for a salad.

Makes 24

INGREDIENTS

12 medium eggs

1¾ cups (350 grams) pickled beets (juice reserved)

2 tablespoons Dijon mustard

1 tablespoon smoked paprika

1½ teaspoons cayenne pepper

Generous pinch of salt

Chives or spring onions, finely chopped, for garnish

METHOD

1. Half fill a medium to large saucepan with water and bring to a boil. Reduce the heat so it simmers and carefully place the eggs in the pan, one at a time, using a slotted spoon.

2. Simmer, uncovered, for 10 minutes. Meanwhile, prepare a large bowl with ice-cold water and have this standing by.

3. Once done, remove the eggs with a slotted spoon and plunge them straight into the bowl of cold water. Leave them for at least 5 minutes while you prepare the beets.

4. Drain the juice from your jar of beets into a large sealable container. Set the beets themselves aside.

5. Carefully peel the cooled eggs; doing this while they're still submerged in the water should make it easier.

6. Place the peeled eggs in the beet juice, cover the container, and place it in the fridge for at least 2 hours or overnight. The juice is unlikely to fully cover them, so turn them a few times during the process.

7. Meanwhile, make a purée by combining the beets, mustard, spices, and salt in a blender (or use a large bowl and hand blender) and blitzing until smooth.

8. Once the eggs are suitably pink, carefully halve them, lengthwise, and scoop out the yolks. Mash these well with a fork in a medium bowl before adding to the beet purée and mixing well.

9. Place the halved eggs on a paper towel and pat dry to remove excess moisture and arrange them on a serving platter or plates. (If making in advance, use any tray or chopping board for this step.)

10. Spoon the beet mixture into a piping bag with a medium to large nozzle and carefully pipe swirls on the eggs, starting by filling the gap left by the yolks and moving between each egg until the mixture is used up. (It will be roughly double the height of the egg.)

11. You can store the eggs overnight in the fridge, in airtight containers (taking care not to smudge the filling). When ready to serve, sprinkle them with chives or spring onions.

Herb and Cheese Egg-Bread

News of Willie, Doctor Copeland's son and a former worker at the New York Café, shakes everyone to the core. Mick Kelly, instantly and irrevocably haunted by the news, desperately tries to console the doctor with hot coffee. Doctor Copeland's daughter, Portia, meanwhile, implores him to stay and eat "a good hot meal" with her rather than making house calls. On the menu is a comforting trio of fried fish, potatoes, and "egg-bread."

Often known as Southern buttermilk corn bread, egg-bread is a fluffier, spoonable variation of corn bread, served as a side to mop up sauces or split, like a sandwich, and filled with creamed chicken.

This savory egg-bread recipe is laced with chili flakes, herbs, and chunks of cheese. It's delicious served in hunks with chili, stews, and hearty bean soups or just eaten as it is.

Serves 8

INGREDIENTS

2 cups (500 milliliters) buttermilk or whole milk
Juice of ½ lemon (if using whole milk)
Slightly less than 2 cups (300 grams) polenta
½ teaspoon baking soda
1 cup (100 grams) cheddar, grated
1 teaspoon chili flakes
1 tablespoon finely chopped fresh rosemary
1 tablespoon finely chopped fresh thyme
Pinch of salt
3 medium eggs

METHOD

1. Preheat the oven to 390°F/200°C/180°C fan/gas mark 6. Grease a 9-inch (23-centimeter) square ovenproof dish.

2. If using whole milk, make a buttermilk substitute: pour the milk into a jug and add the lemon juice. Leave for around 10 minutes, or until it starts to thicken and smells slightly sour, then give it a whisk.

3. Place this mixture, or the buttermilk, into a large saucepan and warm over low to medium heat. Once hot but not boiling, remove from the heat and add the polenta, baking soda, cheese, chili flakes, herbs, and salt, whisking to combine.

4. Using a stand mixer or by hand in a small bowl, whisk the eggs until thick and fluffy, then gradually add them to the polenta mixture, beating with a wooden spoon to combine.

5. Pour into your greased dish and bake for half an hour, until puffed up, golden, and firm to the touch, with no more than a slight wobble. If it needs a little longer, put it back in the oven for 5 minutes at a time, covering loosely with foil if it starts to look too brown.

6. Allow it to cool slightly before cutting into squares or scooping straight onto plates.

Chocolate Porter Ice Cream

IT'S HARD TO imagine a sweeter, or sadder, treat than the one Mick orders at the New York Café. Half crumpled with grief, she decides that some ice cream might make her feel OK. She wants herself "a chocolate sundae and a nickel glass of draw beer," an order that perfectly encapsulates her position on the cusp of adulthood.

This recipe combines the classic chocolate ice cream of childhood with the bittersweet taste of porter, and it's perfect for our sundae recipe, below.

Serves 6 to 8

INGREDIENTS

2 cups (500 milliliters) heavy cream
1 cup (250 milliliters) porter or stout
4 ounces (100 grams) dark chocolate, broken into small pieces
6 egg yolks
½ cup (100 grams) granulated sugar

METHOD

1. Place the cream and porter in a medium saucepan and warm over low heat, whisking continuously.

2. Once hot but not boiling, add the chocolate and continue to whisk for 10 to 15 minutes, until it's melted and there are no flecks. Remove from the heat.

3. In a medium bowl whisk the egg yolks with the sugar for a few minutes, so they're pale and a little fluffy.

4. Add a little of the chocolate cream mixture to the eggs, whisking as you do, then pour the mixture back into the saucepan.

5. Return the pan to low to medium heat and stir continuously until it has the texture of custard and coats the back of the spoon.

6. Remove the pan from the heat and allow the mixture to cool before transferring it to a lidded tub. Refrigerate for 2 to 3 hours, until the mixture is well chilled.

7. Churn the mixture in your ice cream maker, according to instructions, before returning to a tub and freezing for 4 hours or overnight. If you don't have an ice cream maker, freeze the ice cream in the tub or a shallow pan for 4 hours, stirring with a fork every 45 minutes or so.

8. Remove from the freezer 15 to 20 minutes before serving to soften.

Mick's Sad Sundae

MICK IS A complex sundae of sorts—but the way her luck's going, probably without the cherry on top. Predictably, the ice cream creation and even the glass of beer aren't enough to pull her from the doldrums she finds herself in, with the sundae being described as just "O.K., covered all over with chocolate and nuts and cherries."

We suspect it's her mood, rather than the sundae itself, that's the issue. This recipe, starting with our Chocolate Porter Ice Cream (or any ice cream you like) and topped with a chocolate salted caramel sauce, cherries, nuts, and whipped cream, is an absolute delight—and guaranteed to bring at least a little cheer.

In the spirit of solitary solidarity, this recipe serves one person, though it can be easily scaled up if you are in the mood for company. If not, store your extra sauce in the fridge or freezer, on hand for when you next need a boost.

Serves 1

INGREDIENTS

Sauce (enough for 4 sundaes)

⅓ cup (75 grams) muscovado or other dark sugar
3½ tablespoons (50 grams) butter
⅔ cup (150 milliliters) heavy cream
¼ teaspoon flaky sea salt
2 ounces (50 grams) dark chocolate, broken into small pieces

Sundae

3–4 fresh cherries, destoned and quartered
½ teaspoon superfine sugar
5 tablespoons (75 milliliters) whipping or heavy cream
2–3 scoops Chocolate Porter Ice Cream (page 94) or any of your choice
1 teaspoon chopped hazelnuts
1 whole cherry, to garnish

METHOD

1. For the sauce, place all the ingredients, except the chocolate, into a small saucepan and bring to a simmer over low to medium heat, stirring until the butter has melted and the sugar has dissolved. Cook for a further minute and remove from the heat.

2. To melt the chocolate, bring a large saucepan of water to a simmer. Set a heatproof bowl over the pan, making sure the water isn't touching the bottom of the bowl. Add the chocolate and stir with a wooden spoon until melted.

3. Pour in the sauce mixture and stir to combine, then remove it from the heat and allow it to cool.

4. In a small bowl, toss the cherries with the sugar and set aside.

5. In a medium bowl or stand mixer, whip the cream to soft peaks and set aside.

6. To assemble the sundae, scoop ice cream into a bowl or sundae glass, spoon over the cherries, top with the cream, and pour over as much sauce as you'd like. Sprinkle over the nuts and put a cherry on top.

8

A Hungry Home and Stiff Suppers in Shirley Jackson's *The Haunting of Hill House*

FOOD TASTES FUNNY, AND INGREDIENTS ECHO A WORLD SOMEWHERE BEYOND A HAUNTED HOUSE IN JACKSON'S SEMINAL NOVEL.

FROM THE EARLIEST pages of Shirley Jackson's great Gothic ghost story, the domestic is upturned: a house is described as "not sane"; another home is besieged by "showers of stones"; groceries spill and splatter onto pavements and roll into the gutter; a little girl speaks mysteriously of her "cup of stars."

For Eleanor, one of three strangers brought to Hill House as part of a paranormal experiment, passing a cozy-looking home prompts fantasies of being cared for and coddled with meals a child might invent ("a bird, and radishes from the garden" and lashings of homemade plum jam).

Jackson employs food as a classic Gothic device, using it to hint that something else is going on beneath the surface. Something seems (or tastes) a little off here; things are not quite what they appear or are supposed to be.

Embodying all of this, and in some ways more terrifying than the house, is Mrs. Dudley (described by Luke, another of the chosen trio, in an apt metaphor, as having a "face of curds"). On the surface, Hill House's cook has all the qualities of the maternal, nurturing figure Eleanor longs for (one who will happily care for her but never become a bother). She bakes (and makes a mean soufflé). She prepares generous breakfast spreads and appears to go out of her way to source the best ingredients for everything she cooks. She ensures that everyone is well fed at all times and no meal is ever missed.

But it's in her insistence on the guests eating at set times every day, and the increasingly luxurious dishes she creates, that we begin to find latent horror.

Mrs. Dudley and her husband, who is Hill House's caretaker, have been there forever, it seems. They've seen people come and go (or should that be, come and stay forever?). So their behavior, from Mr. Dudley's general avoidance of the group to Mrs. Dudley's impenetrable demeanor and robotic conversation, offers an indication that this haunted house business might be more than just a bit of a lark.

The generosity and warmth of Mrs. Dudley's cooking isn't reflected in her manner. How can someone so chilly prepare such decadent desserts, and how can a nervous cook make a good soufflé (which, to third experimentee Theodora, is impossible)? More to the point, and perhaps even more befuddling, why *doesn't* she seem nervous, amid such eerie goings-on?

Her actions certainly suggest that she knows something the guests do not. She leaves before dark, once she's laid out the dinner. Her kitchen has more doors than could possibly be required. Just what, wonders Eleanor, is Mrs. Dudley "in the habit of meeting in her kitchen" that means she needs a swift escape?

Doors become, like the house as a whole, alive, confusing the guests and trapping them in a mind-boggling maze. There are doors everywhere: doors to somewhere, doors to nowhere, even trap doors. Theodora and Eleanor get lost looking for breakfast, in a panic because (of course) Mrs. Dudley clears everything away at "ten o'clock." When they eventually reach the dining room, after passing through several dark, unfamiliar spaces, Dr. Montague says he left the doors open; they closed themselves.

Mrs. Dudley is determinedly unamused by the situation and unsympathetic to their lateness. She refuses conversation, repeating, in response to Luke's continuous chatter and questioning, that she has to get the breakfast dishes back on the shelves before taking them out again for lunch at one o'clock. Is this stubborn schedule at Mrs. Dudley's insistence, we wonder, or is she merely an agent of the house? Why must the dishes be so promptly reshelved before being removed again, and what would happen if they weren't? It's as if she also has a mealtime schedule for the house and its maw (masquerading as a shelf) has to be fed with crockery.

The housekeeper's rigidity, whatever the reason for it, takes on a more sinister edge as the pages turn.

The kitchen, thanks to its overseer and those drafty-sounding doors, feels rather chilly for the heart of the home. It should feel warm and fragrant with all that baking, but Jackson's descriptions strip away any sense of comfort and coziness.

Suppers, too, lack conviviality, despite the eclectic and rather eccentric bunch of guests and despite the delicious dishes served by Mrs. Dudley. "Food has a different flavor," muses Dr. Montague. Luke agrees, relieved that he isn't the only one to have noticed it. (Neither man, though, can quite pinpoint how or why.)

The statement echoes Eleanor's odd announcement earlier; discussing the prospect of a soufflé for supper, she confides that her mother's kitchen was "dark and narrow" and nothing cooked there had any taste or color. (Eleanor, as we learn right from the start, has never known domestic bliss.)

At Hill House, though, there is taste and color, and the flavors are far from unpleasant. In fact, Mrs. Dudley's meals are invariably described as admirable. She is, as Mrs. Montague observes, "a fine cook." And doesn't that just make it all the creepier? We feel that they are under a spell, that they are being coddled in a twisted version of Eleanor's fantasy of a dainty old lady preparing birds, radishes, and plum jam.

A rather jolly-sounding peach shortcake seems like something that should be served by a grandmother with a warm hug, rather than an indifferent housekeeper with a cold shoulder. It's this dessert that has Eleanor wondering about the world outside and, in fact, whether there still is one at all. Mrs. Dudley gives nothing away (at least, not in words), and this lack of meaningful contact with anyone who steps beyond the gates of Hill House exacerbates the feeling that they are incarcerated here.

Eleanor's obsession with the heavy cream and peaches, and where Mrs. Dudley might possibly find them, highlights the characters' odd situation. They are mesmerized by the house, by its caretakers, and by the food served within it. As their grip on reality loosens, Hill House's grip on them pulls ever tighter (as, we might assume from the sheer amount they are eating, do their clothes). The familiar framework of mealtimes has become a frightening trap that keeps them in the house, even though they're too afraid to clear away the dirty dinner dishes (no one wants to go into the kitchen alone, with all those doors!).

The great outdoors provides no comfort. A family picnic, typically a scene that conjures pure, unadulterated joy, has Theodora and Eleanor fleeing from the checked tablecloth and "bright fruit" in terror. Their earlier fantasies of idyllic picnics with chicken salad, chocolate cake, lemonade, and "spilled salt" have been subverted once again by Hill House. It's especially tragic for Eleanor, so hungry for familial connections and the childhood she never had.

When the group wants more coffee (after ten o'clock, if you please), no one wants to challenge Mrs. Dudley's rigid rules. Volunteered for the job by Dr. Montague, Luke jokes that the cook is "perfectly capable of a *filet de Luke à la meunière.*" It feels very close to the bone, indeed, when, by this point in the novel, we have a growing sense that these guests are being fattened up, Hansel and Gretel style.

Drawn in by the deliciousness of the food, they continue to gorge themselves even as their suspicions grow, with Eleanor even suggesting that Hill House wants "to consume us, take us into itself, make us part [of it]."

Perhaps it isn't the guests Mrs. Dudley is really feeding after all—but, instead, a very hungry house.

A Bird, and Radishes from the Garden

ELEANOR IS RATHER given to flights of fancy, and cozy, comforting food features heavily. As she draws closer to Hill House, she passes a home that (we have to assume) is rather less sinister—somewhere she might be happy, perhaps, rather than the embodiment of pure evil. She imagines living her days out there in contentment, being waited on by a "little dainty old lady" who brings her elderberry wine, for health's sake, and sets the table for her solo supper: "I dined upon a bird, and radishes from the garden."

It's a scene dripping with dramatic irony and shadowed by impending doom, as we (even as first-time readers) already have an inkling that the house she's headed to isn't quite so benevolent.

Eleanor's quaint little imaginary supper inspires our recipe of spatchcock chicken, smothered in a peppery, zingy pesto made with radish tops (save the radishes for our Radish Remoulade, page 104) before roasting for flavor-infused, tender meat. Ask your butcher to spatchcock the chicken for you or follow the steps outlined below.

This is also a lovely recipe to cook on the barbecue (use skewers to hold the chicken together) and will work well with watercress if you can't find radish tops or if the bunch isn't quite full enough.

Serves 4

INGREDIENTS

1 medium chicken (around 3.3 pounds or 1.5 kilograms)

Radish-Top Pesto

Leafy tops from a large bunch of radishes (around 6⅔ cups or 200 grams greens)

¾ cups (100 grams) pine nuts

3 cloves garlic

2 cups (50 grams) basil

¾ cups (200 milliliters) olive oil

Juice of 1 lemon

1½ cups (150 grams) Parmesan, divided

METHOD

1. To spatchcock the chicken, place it, breast side down, on a clean cutting board. Using a pair of sharp, clean scissors, cut along one side of the backbone, starting at the tail end and cutting up to the neck.

2. Repeat on the other side of the backbone and remove it. Open the chicken out and turn it over, then use the heel of your hand to firmly press down and flatten the chicken, breaking the breastbone. Continue to flatten so the meat is pretty much the same thickness throughout.

3. Preheat the oven to 390°F/200°C/180°C fan/gas mark 6. To make the radish-top pesto, in a colander, rinse the radish tops thoroughly, removing any dirt, then gently squeeze out the excess water and place them on a paper towel to drain.

4. Place the pine nuts and garlic in a food processor and blitz roughly for a few seconds, then add the radish tops, basil, oil, lemon juice, and half of the Parmesan. Blitz again until smooth, then stir in the remaining Parmesan.

5. Place the chicken, skin side up, on a large baking sheet and spread it with the pesto, covering evenly. Roast, uncovered, for 45 minutes to an hour, until the juices run clear when you insert a skewer or sharp knife.

6. Remove the chicken from the oven, loosely cover with foil, and rest for 10 to 15 minutes before carving.

Radish Remoulade

Hopefully, Eleanor's imaginary grandmother figure/servant isn't one to waste food. We certainly aren't—hence this recipe. This remoulade uses up the radishes after their frilly green tops have been lopped off for the pesto in our recipe above and happens to go beautifully with the chicken too.

This is generally a lovely side dish for a barbecue or any al fresco meal, and it's easy to make a vegan version; just use nondairy yogurt, like coconut, in place of the mayonnaise.

Serves 4 to 6

INGREDIENTS

1 celery root, regular size
1 bunch radishes (around 2 cups or 250 grams)
7 tablespoons mayonnaise or yogurt
3 tablespoons Dijon mustard
Juice of 2 lemons
Salt and freshly ground black pepper

METHOD

1. Peel the celery root and coarsely grate half of it. Cut the other half into very thin matchsticks. Place both in a large mixing bowl.

2. Halve the radishes, then slice them very thinly, so they form half-moon shapes. Add them to the bowl.

3. Add the mayonnaise, mustard, and lemon juice to a separate small bowl and whisk with a fork to blend.

4. Pour the dressing over the celery root and radishes and mix well to ensure an even coating throughout. Season well with salt and pepper.

Homemade Plum Jam

Eleanor's imaginary dinner of "a bird, and radishes from the garden" is, incongruously, accompanied by homemade plum jam. It's telling of her character: selfish, needy, rather childlike, and prone to fantasy. She wants to be looked after, though the old lady she imagines tending to her fades into the background, delivering meals with a ghostly benevolence. Her dinner also feels like a mosaic of childhood memories, rather than an actual meal.

Nonetheless, there's something wonderfully warm and comforting about homemade jam, especially when spiced with fragrant cardamom. We wouldn't recommend eating it with a bird and radishes, though it is rather nice on toast. For a less sweet version, which can be enjoyed with cold meats and cheeses, reduce the sugar by a third and replace the cardamom with 1 teaspoon of chili flakes.

Fills 2 medium jam jars (1¼ to 2 cups [300 to 480 grams] of jam)

INGREDIENTS

4½ cups (800 grams) plums (overripe is fine)
4 tablespoons water
4¼ cups (800 grams) granulated sugar or jam sugar
Juice of ½ lemon
2 cardamom pods, lightly crushed
1 tablespoon (15 grams) butter

METHOD

1. Preheat the oven to 320°F/160°C/140°C fan/gas mark 3 and boil a pot of water. First, sterilize your jam jars—it's worth having one extra, in case there's a little jam to spare. Clean the jars, lids, and rubber seals, if using, with warm, soapy water and rinse thoroughly.

2. Place only the jars on a baking sheet lined with parchment paper, facing upward, and dry them in the oven for around 10 minutes. Meanwhile,

place the lids and rubber seals in a bowl and cover them with the boiling water, fishing them out after around 10 minutes. Set these aside while you make the jam.

3. Halve the plums and carefully remove the stones, using your fingers or a small, sharp knife. Chop them roughly and add them to a large saucepan with the water. Place the pan over medium heat and bring the mixture to a simmer, cooking for around 10 minutes, or until the fruit is tender and just starting to fall apart.

4. Add the sugar, lemon juice, and cardamom pods (or any spices you like), stir well, and return to low heat, stirring occasionally for 10 to 15 minutes, until the sugar dissolves.

5. Increase the heat and bring to a rapid boil until it reaches 220°F/105°C. (Use a sugar thermometer to test; if you don't have one, drop a small amount into a glass of cold water. If it forms a ball you can fish out, it's ready.) This should take 5 to 10 minutes.

6. Remove the pan from the heat, stir in the butter, and fish out the cardamom pods. Allow the jam to cool for 15 minutes or so before pouring into your sterilized and cooled jars. Place a circle of parchment paper on top before sealing and leave for at least 24 hours before eating.

Spooky Soufflé

MRS. DUDLEY'S SUPERIOR soufflé is something of a mystery in itself, seeing as (as Theodora confidently points out): "A nervous cook can't make a good soufflé, anyone knows that."

Mrs. Dudley has every reason to be nervous. She lives in a house where nothing moves, except from the corner of one's eye. Her kitchen is the heart of a warren, with a disproportionate number of doors leading to the veranda (doors the cook seems eager to keep firmly closed). The house she works in has been occupied by a team of paranormal investigators (albeit amateur).

Yet she still manages to produce what Dr. Montague declares is "an admirable soufflé." Spooky, indeed.

We've taken the classic cheese soufflé and added the sweet earthiness (and Halloween connotations) of roast pumpkin or butternut squash. You can also use canned pumpkin—skip ahead to step 3 and flash-fry the sage leaves in a little oil before adding them. The resulting individual soufflés should be puffy and golden (it's natural if some patches darken more than others) and make for a wonderful supper with a tossed green salad and intriguing company.

Serves 4

INGREDIENTS

1 medium butternut squash or a small pumpkin

6–8 sage leaves

2 tablespoons olive oil

Salt and freshly ground black pepper

1⅔ cups (400 milliliters) whole milk

3 tablespoons all-purpose flour

2¾ tablespoons (40 grams) butter

⅔ cup (75 grams) cheddar or a mix of cheddar and Parmesan, grated

2 tablespoons of butter

4 eggs, separated

METHOD

1. Preheat the oven to 390°F/200°C/180°C fan/gas mark 6. Peel and halve the butternut squash, scoop out the seeds, and roughly chop the flesh into medium-sized cubes.

2. Place the squash in a roasting pan with the sage leaves, drizzle over the olive oil, and sprinkle with a little salt. Roast for 40 to 45 minutes, shaking the pan a couple of times during cooking, until the squash is tender. Remove the sage and set it aside to cool slightly.

3. Transfer the squash (or pumpkin, if using) to a blender, or to a large bowl if using a hand blender, and blitz it to a fairly smooth purée (don't worry about the odd lumpy bit). Set this aside to cool while you make a cheese sauce.

4. In a medium saucepan, combine the milk, flour, and butter and place over medium heat, whisking continuously for 5 to 6 minutes, until it forms a sauce that generously coats the back of a spoon, like a thick custard.

5. Remove from the heat, whisk in the cheese, and season to taste with salt and pepper. Allow the sauce to cool to room temperature before combining with the purée.

6. Preheat the oven to 350°F/180°C/160°C fan/gas mark 4. Use the butter to grease four ovenproof soufflé bowls, cups, or mugs, each with a capacity of around 1¼ to 1¾ cups (300–400 milliliters), and arrange them on a baking sheet.

7. Add the egg yolks to the sauce and squash mixture, beating well to combine.

8. In a large clean, dry bowl or stand mixer, whisk the egg whites to form stiff peaks. Add a couple of tablespoons to the mixture and beat, then (ideally using a metal spoon or a spatula) carefully fold in the rest, a little at a time. You're aiming for a smooth, still airy mix, similar to a mousse.

9. Divide the mixture between your prepared vessels and pop them in the center of the hot oven, baking for 20 to 25 minutes, until puffy, golden, and still a little wobbly (peek through the oven door, if you can, as opening it during cooking can cause the soufflés to sag). Serve immediately.

Mrs. Dudley's Peach Shortcakes

JACKSON'S NOVEL TAKES the domestic and gives it a demonic edge. Never is this clearer than in the moments, and meals, that should be cozy and comforting yet ring some distant, muffled warning bell.

Mrs. Dudley evokes this slightly off-kilter feeling by her very presence; she insists on following a timetable of meals to the dot, leaving for "somewhere else" each day while the others are trapped by Hill House and its mysterious, increasingly malignant ways.

Take these delicious peach shortcakes, a sunshine-infused picnic or teatime treat that should spark joy. For Eleanor, they prompt her to wonder, "Is there still a world somewhere?" So firm has the building's grip become on her psyche that she is startled to consider that the heavy cream and peaches have been sourced from beyond its walls.

Serves 8

INGREDIENTS

1⅔ cups (200 grams) all-purpose flour
⅓ cup (75 grams) superfine sugar
¼ teaspoon salt
¼ teaspoon baking soda
1 teaspoon baking powder
⅓ cup (75 grams) butter, fridge cold and cubed
⅓ cups (100 grams) full-fat yogurt
1 egg, beaten
A little brown sugar, to sprinkle

Peach Compote

3–4 peaches, sliced
1 tablespoon clear honey
1 tablespoon water
Sprig of thyme (optional)
¾ cups (200 milliliters) heavy cream, to serve

METHOD

1. Preheat the oven to 390°F/200°C/180°C fan/gas mark 6. Place all the dry ingredients (except the brown sugar) in a large bowl and mix, then rub the butter in with your fingertips to reach the texture of fine breadcrumbs (as with a crumble). Fold in the yogurt and egg with a spatula or wooden spoon until well mixed. It will hold together but will be quite wet, like cake batter.

2. Butter a muffin or cupcake pan and divide the mixture into eight (roughly a heaped dessert spoon in each cell). Sprinkle the tops with a little brown sugar and bake the shortcakes for 15 to 20 minutes, until just lightly golden and firm to the touch. Cool them in the pan for 10 minutes and then turn them out onto a wire rack.

3. To make the compote, place all of the ingredients (saving some peach slices to decorate, if you like) in a medium-sized saucepan and gently heat until the honey and water dissolve together to form a light syrup.

4. Simmer gently for 10 to 15 minutes, agitating the pan occasionally to prevent sticking. It's ready once the peaches are tender and just starting to break down yet still holding their shape. Set aside.

5. In a large bowl whip the cream to form soft peaks. Slice the shortcakes in half, spoon the still-warm peaches on the bottoms, layer with cream, top with a few fresh peach slices, and finish with the shortcake tops.

Salmon with Caper Sauce

FOR THE MOTLEY crew assembled at Hill House, the arrival of Mrs. Montague and her rather rude companion, headmaster Arthur Parker, is as irritating as the atmosphere is terrifying. Their brusque comments and interference (including séances with the use of a planchette) have the others longing to return to their haunted existence in relative peace.

Dr. Montague, who (Eleanor observes) seems uncomfortable in his wife's presence, tries to warm up the atmosphere with jovial conversation and good food, including Mrs. Dudley's caper sauce. It's so good that, as she "daintily" has a taste, Mrs. Montague is moved to pronounce, "You have found a fair cook, have you not?"

It's a natural match for fish, crisped in a frying pan before the ingredients for the zesty, piquant sauce are added. You can use any fish fillets, like sea bass or lemon sole, and it's delicious served with new potatoes and greens, with the sauce coating everything with a buttery drizzle. Rice and salad are equally cozy companions.

Serves 2

INGREDIENTS

2 fillets of salmon, skin on

Salt and freshly ground black pepper

1 tablespoon extra-virgin olive oil

2 tablespoons (or a good glug) white wine

Juice and zest of 1 lemon

2 tablespoons capers

1 tablespoon (15 grams) butter

2 tablespoons finely chopped flat-leaf parsley, to serve

METHOD

1. Pat the fillets dry and season the skin and flesh with salt and pepper. Place the olive oil in a large hot pan over medium-high heat.

2. Once the oil is sizzling, place the fish skin-side down. Cook the fish for 2 to 3 minutes, until the skin is crisp and the flesh is turning opaque. Press down gently with a spatula as it cooks—you can lift it up slightly to check progress.

3. Flip the fish, then add the wine. Allow it to bubble for a minute, then add the lemon juice and zest, capers, and butter. Add a little more salt and pepper, if you like.

4. Bring the sauce to a bubble, reduce the heat to medium-low, and cook the fish for 1 to 2 minutes, until it is cooked through. Throw on the chopped parsley and serve.

9

The Food of Witchcraft, and Neighbors from Hell, in Ira Levin's *Rosemary's Baby*

THE DEVIL'S IN THE DOMESTIC, AND PROBABLY IN THE PUDDING, TOO, IN A NOVEL THAT BRINGS THE GOTHIC VERY CLOSE TO HOME.

NEIGHBORS SHARING FOOD is nothing new. Whether it's breaking bread together, borrowing a cup of sugar, or bringing around a casserole following a bereavement, food and community are intertwined. These are gestures of goodwill and baby steps toward friendship.

Not for Rosemary, however. Ira Levin's 1967 novel—and Roman Polanski's film adaptation, released the following year—takes neighborly kindness and twists it, tightly, in myriad dark directions.

The signs are ominous from the start. As Rosemary and Guy, newly wed and superficially happy, secure their apartment in a posh New York block, their friend gives them a little history. This was, he tells them, where the cannibalistic Trench sisters "performed their little dietary experiments"—cooking and eating children. Already, the domestic setting is tainted and blood soaked, while food and consumption are linked to evil and the destruction of innocence.

Guy finds this *most* amusing, while, aside from a moment's pause over her melon starter, Rosemary also chooses to shrug off the story. She quickly places herself in a role we've seen many times in Gothic literature: that of the unsuspecting female protagonist manipulated into a terrible fate.

The novel plays upon our most intimate fears of betrayal, contamination of the body, and oppression by potent forces of evil. And all this happens insidiously, through food, from a chocolate mousse to an insipid green milkshake.

Food is how the eccentric but far from harmless Roman and Minnie Castevet worm their way into Guy and Rosemary's lives. Like vampires, they're invited in, largely out of politeness. Once they've elbowed their way through the apartment door, each casserole, luridly green smoothie, and chocolate "mouse" they deliver pulls Rosemary further into a terrible trap.

The couple's first meal in the apartment is an innocent picnic of tuna sandwiches and beer, a romantic celebration interrupted by the braying sounds of their new neighbors. Soon they see them, too, as Minnie comes around for coffee and cake. Her refusal to "let Rosemary disturb the living-room on her account" is another subtle hint at the diabolical creeping into the domestic realm—spaces are personified, looming large and sinister. Earlier, Rosemary is hysterically happy at the size of the kitchen, with its "mammoth refrigerator" and "monumental sink."

It's not long until she loses control over these spaces and the food prepared, served, and eaten within them.

Take that chocolate mousse, for example. In one of the most famous scenes, Minnie once again interrupts a romantic celebration to bring two "custard cups" with (says Guy, mimicking their neighbor's accent) "chocolate mouse."

The description of the mousse is, on the surface, delicious. Each cup has "peaked swirls of chocolate," while Guy's is topped with chopped nuts and Rosemary's with a half walnut. This latter isn't incidental—in witchcraft, walnuts symbolize unity and fertility. The Castevets have plans for Rosemary—and her womb.

Rosemary's suspicions are aroused by a "chalky undertaste," which Guy dismisses as "silly, honey." He guilts her into eating it, mentioning how the "old bat" must have slaved away making it and, oddly, mentioning another sinister gift to Rosemary from the Castevets: a tannis root charm. The uncanny is creeping in, revealing the unfamiliar in the familiar; suddenly, Rosemary is protecting herself from her husband by sneaking spoonfuls of uneaten mousse into a napkin. ("'There, Daddy,' she said, tilting the cup towards him. 'Do I get a gold star on my chart?'")

This scene brings the most overt evidence yet of the Castevets' unnatural, dangerous obsession with Rosemary and gives us an insight into how Guy controls his wife. He, too, appears to be falling under the Castevets' witchy spells and is now complicit in their plans.

Guy's controlling nature has already shown itself. Rosemary admits to not understanding some of his references (he's nine years older than her and a rather pretentious struggling actor), and he often infantilizes her with patronizing comments under the guise of humor. "Did you eat your egg?" he asks. "Did you eat your Captain Crunch?" And in an earlier scene featuring devilish desserts, Guy's consumption of two slices of homemade Boston cream pie, despite its "peculiar and unpleasant sweetness," has her wondering whether she can trust him; is he acting?

Even for (first-time) readers, there's a lurking shadow of doubt: is Rosemary descending into madness and tasting something that isn't there? Or is there really a sinister plot afoot? If the latter, she is surrounded by actors, with friends, neighbors, and even Guy—the person she should trust the most—conspiring to trap her.

From the mousse (or mouse) onward, Rosemary's body is no longer her own. Her appetite follows its own narrative arc, from those simple apartment picnics (she finds comfort in childlike pleasures) to mainlining "man-size cans of beef stew and chilli con carne," a sign that she is pregnant.

But her appetite dwindles, and rather than cravings she has "an aversion to salt." Understandably, Rosemary is beginning to mistrust food while another force is taking over her body. Soon, she needs only a single vegetable and a "small piece of rare meat" for dinner.

She obligingly drinks the "cold and sour" watery pistachio milkshake Minnie brings to her each day. At least, it *looks* like a watery pistachio milkshake. What's actually in it remains a mystery. "Snips and snails and puppy-dogs' tails," Minnie jokes (or perhaps not). A snippet of their agenda is revealed here: this baby must be a boy.

The mother no longer seems to matter; she has become passive. No longer does Rosemary hide food and complain about strange tastes. She drains her glass obediently, even while seeming rather disgusted by the contents. She takes to eating meat that's nearly raw, "broiled only long enough to take away the refrigerator's chill and seal the juices." She even gnaws on a raw chicken heart, catching her reflection in the toaster and seeing a woman possessed.

It prompts a rebellion of sorts, and it takes place in the kitchen. Rosemary decides to take back control of the domestic sphere, hosting a dinner party with a menu copied from the pages of a cookbook named *Life*—suggesting that she is clinging to a normal life with her fingertips. This time, she tips Minnie's shake down the sink, instead downing a not-very-baby-friendly concoction of egg, sugar, and sherry.

It all falls apart when she sheds tears into the salad, giving it an "extra zing." Overcome with guilt over the boozy drink and resigned to her fate, she is now completely at the mercy of her neighbors, their sinister circle, and her own husband. Even a "successful chupe" (Chilean seafood stew) can't save her now.

Chicken Marengo

HAVING MADE A fateful move into her new apartment with Guy, and in full nesting mode, Rosemary is fleetingly "busy and happy." Or perhaps she is distracting herself from the feeling of dread that has already, at the start of chapter 3, begun to tiptoe into her consciousness. Among her distractions is cooking for Guy: "chicken Marengo and vitello tonnato," followed by "a mocha layer cake and a jarful of butter cookies."

A French-Italian dish of chicken simmered in a tomato sauce that's been laced with wine and brandy, it's named after the 1800 Battle of Marengo. The recipe was, popular legend has it, created on the hoof by Napoleon Bonaparte's chef, who needed to rustle up a meal for the victorious leader and used whatever he had on hand, which included stolen chickens, tomatoes, herbs, and a clutch of eggs, which were fried and served on top of the dish. We haven't included the eggs in this recipe, though it certainly isn't a bad idea to turn this dish into a brunch feast.

Serves 4

INGREDIENTS

2 tablespoons (30 grams) butter

2 tablespoons olive oil

4 chicken legs or thighs, skin on

3 cups (200 grams) mushrooms, thinly sliced

1 onion, finely chopped

2 cloves garlic, minced

1 bay leaf

2 sprigs fresh thyme, or ½ teaspoon dried
½ cup (100 milliliters) white wine (optional)
3 tablespoons brandy (optional)
14 ounces (400 grams) canned tomatoes, diced
2 tablespoons tomato purée
½ cup (100 milliliters) chicken stock (⅔ cup or 150 milliliters, if not adding wine)
2 sprigs fresh flat-leaf parsley
Freshly ground black pepper

METHOD

1. Place the butter and oil in a large pan over medium heat. Once hot, add the chicken. Cook for around 5 minutes on each side, so it's well browned.

2. Add the mushrooms, onion, garlic, bay leaf, and thyme and cook for a further 5 minutes. Add the wine and brandy, if using, then turn up the heat and allow the mixture to bubble for a couple of minutes.

3. Give everything a stir, then add the tomatoes, tomato purée, stock, parsley, and a little pepper.

4. Bring it back to a boil, then simmer over low heat for 25 to 30 minutes, until the chicken is cooked through and tender and the sauce coats the back of a spoon. Serve with crusty bread or mashed potatoes and green vegetables.

Homemade Boston Cream Pie

The creepy Castevets' Boston cream pie gives an early clue as to what they're up to. Rosemary detects "a peculiar and unpleasant sweetness," while Guy demolishes two slices.

The devil is clearly in the dessert, though Boston cream pie itself—more accurately a cake—is rather heavenly. This cream-filled, chocolate-covered sponge cake was created at Boston's Parker House in 1856 and remains a staple dessert at the hotel, typically iced with dark and white chocolate and edged with toasted sliced almonds.

It's likely that the Castevets made theirs with the Betty Crocker cake mix that popularized this dessert in the 1950s (probably adding a few secret and sinister ingredients of their own).

Ours is a simplified version of the original, with a luxuriously thick crème pâtissière sandwiched between light-as-air sponge cake, glazed with a silky ganache cape.

Serves 10 *to* 12

INGREDIENTS

Crème Pâtissière

⅓ cup (75 grams) granulated sugar
3 tablespoons cornstarch
4 eggs
1½ tablespoons (20 grams) butter
3⅛ cups (750 milliliters) whole milk
1 teaspoon dark rum, or ½ teaspoon rum flavoring (optional)

Sponge

4 eggs
¾ cups (150 grams) granulated sugar
1¼ cups (150 grams) all-purpose flour
1 teaspoon baking powder

Glaze

3.5 ounces (100 grams) dark chocolate
⅔ cup (150 milliliters) heavy cream
½ teaspoon vanilla extract or paste
Sliced almonds, to decorate (optional)

METHOD

1. First, make the pastry cream (or crème pâtissière). Place the sugar, cornstarch, and eggs in a medium bowl and whisk until fluffy.

2. Add the butter and milk to a medium saucepan and bring to a boil, stirring, over medium heat. Remove from the heat and whisk in the egg mixture, then return the pan to the heat and bring the mixture back to a boil.

3. Simmer for around 5 minutes, whisking continuously, until it's like a very thick custard. Transfer it to a bowl, cover it with parchment paper (so it touches the top of the cream, helping to prevent a skin from forming), and allow it to cool. Chill it in the fridge for 1 to 2 hours or overnight.

4. Meanwhile, to make the sponge, preheat the oven to 350°F/180°C/160°C fan/gas mark 4. Grease and line an 8-inch (20-centimeter) round cake pan.

5. Whisk together the eggs and sugar in a medium bowl with a hand whisk, or in a stand mixer, until thick and fluffy (this will take up to 5 minutes in a stand mixer on medium speed).

6. Sift together the flour and baking powder and gradually add to the wet ingredients, continuing to mix until well combined.

7. Pour the batter into the cake pan and bake for 30 to 35 minutes, until pale golden and springy to the touch. If it looks or feels very wobbly in the middle, return to the oven for 5 minutes at a time, covering loosely if it's starting to look too dark.

8. Allow the cake to cool in the pan for around 5 minutes, then carefully turn it out onto a wire rack to cool completely.

9. Once it's cooled, use a large sharp knife to slice through the middle horizontally to form two layers.

10. Add the rum, if using, to the chilled pastry cream and whisk well for a smooth texture.

11. Arrange the bottom sponge layer on a plate or cake stand and scoop on the pastry cream, reserving 2 tablespoons if you plan to decorate with sliced almonds (see steps 14 and 15). Even out with a frosting spatula, then top with the second cake layer.

12. To make the glaze, place a small heatproof bowl over a pan of simmering water and add the chocolate and cream. Melt, stirring frequently, until well mixed and smooth, then whisk in the vanilla. Set aside, still in the bowl, for around 5 minutes, so it thickens a little.

13. Pour the glaze over the cake so it forms a silky cloak. Allow it to cool.

14. If decorating with sliced almonds, heat a small frying pan over medium heat, then add the almonds and toast for 1 to 2 minutes, tossing the pan frequently, so they're nicely toasted and golden but not burned. Allow them to cool.

15. Use a frosting spatula to spread the reserved pastry cream around the sides of the cake (leaving the top untouched) and press on the toasted almonds.

Stuffed Mushrooms in the Living-Room

A TRAY OF STUFFED mushrooms (and, soon, a bun) in the oven. A typically sullen yet suddenly sunny husband who has finally decided to give Rosemary what she wants (a baby). A couple of Gibsons (martinis garnished with pickled onions) on the go. Some (chalky) mousse soon to be delivered. What could possibly go wrong? Not the mushrooms, if you follow this simple, tasty recipe.

Serve with peppery greens (dressed with olive oil and the juice from the lemon zested for the stuffing) and your retro drink of choice.

Serves 2

INGREDIENTS

4 large portobello mushrooms

1 large slice sourdough bread, slightly stale

Handful of fresh flat-leaf parsley, finely chopped

Handful of fresh mint, finely chopped

1 clove garlic, peeled and finely grated

Zest of 1 lemon

3 tablespoons extra-virgin olive oil

⅓ cup (30 grams) Parmesan, finely grated

METHOD

1. Preheat the oven to 350°F/180°C/160°C fan/gas mark 4. Using a brush or parchment paper, gently clean the mushrooms to remove any soil or grit (there's no need to peel them).

2. Break up the bread, place it in a food processor, and blitz it for rough, medium-fine breadcrumbs.

3. Place the breadcrumbs in a small bowl with the parsley, mint, garlic, and lemon zest and stir to combine. Add the olive oil and stir again to bind everything together.

4. Line a baking sheet with foil or parchment paper. Place the mushrooms skin-side down, and carefully spoon the stuffing mixture onto each mushroom.

5. Top with the Parmesan and bake for 10 to 15 minutes, until the cheese is golden and a little crispy.

Chalk and Chocolate Mousse Cups

"THE MOUSSE WAS excellent, but it had a chalky undertaste that reminded Rosemary of blackboards and grade school."

Dangerous desserts strike again, in one of the most iconic food (and overall) scenes in the novel and movie. Our recipe garnishes individual dark and white chocolate mousses with walnut halves, though you won't find a "chalky undertaste" here ("don't be silly, honey"). If you do, you might want to keep an eye on the neighbors.

Makes 4 individual mousses

INGREDIENTS

Crème Pâtissière

¾ cup (175 milliliters) whole milk

½ vanilla pod

2 egg yolks

2½ tablespoons (30 grams) superfine sugar

¼ cup (30 grams) all-purpose flour, sieved

3 teaspoons powdered gelatin

Mousses

¾ cup (125 grams) dark chocolate chips or smashed/chopped bar

½ cup (75 grams) white chocolate chips or smashed/chopped bar

1 cup (250 milliliters) heavy cream

3 tablespoons Bailey's or other cream liqueur (optional)

Walnut halves, to serve

METHOD

1. To make the crème pâtissière, place the milk and vanilla pod in a heavy-bottomed saucepan and bring to a simmer over low to medium heat, then set aside.

2. In a medium bowl whisk together the egg yolks and sugar, then whisk in the flour.

3. Slowly pour the still-warm milk over the egg mixture, whisking all the while, and return to a clean medium saucepan.

4. Place the pan over medium heat and stir the mixture constantly, making sure it doesn't boil. It's ready when it coats the back of the spoon (usually within a few minutes).

5. Whisk the gelatin into the mixture until dissolved, then remove the pan from the heat.

6. Half fill two large pans with water and bring to a simmer. Place a small heatproof bowl over each, ensuring that they don't touch the water. Add dark chocolate to one bowl and white to the other. Stir each as it melts, then remove from the heat.

7. Add around two-thirds of the crème pâtissière to the dark chocolate and the rest to the white. Add the liqueur, if using, to the white mix. Whisk well to combine and allow to cool to room temperature.

8. In a large bowl whisk the cream to soft, glossy peaks and, using a metal spoon or a spatula, fold two-thirds into the dark chocolate mixture and the rest into the white chocolate mixture.

9. Spoon the dark mousse into teacups, ramekins, or (as in the novel) custard cups, leaving at least 1 centimeter at the top. Top with the white mousse (you can use a piping bag if you want dramatic peaks).

10. Refrigerate for a few hours or overnight, then top each with a walnut half to serve.

Minnie's Milkshake

A CHALKY UNDERTASTE IS one thing, but the drink Minnie shakes up for Rosemary is a little less subtle. She delivers something resembling a "watery pistachio milkshake" each day at 11 a.m., and Rosemary obediently drains it each time, despite its mysterious contents and the fact it's "cold and sour." What's in it? Good question. "Snips and snails and puppy-dogs' tails" is Minnie's reply—and given the Castevets' creepy behavior thus far, that could well be true.

No need to worry about our take on this smoothie: a simple blend of pistachios with lively mint, spinach, and, for a thicker shake, a little avocado.

Serves 1

INGREDIENTS

1 tablespoon pistachios, shelled, plus a few extra, chopped, to serve
1 tablespoon fresh mint leaves
Small handful of spinach leaves
¼ avocado (optional)
1⅔ cups (400 milliliters) milk, divided
Honey or agave syrup, to taste

METHOD

1. Place the pistachios, mint, and spinach in a blender and blitz for around 30 seconds. Add the avocado, if using, and blitz again.

2. Add around a quarter of the milk and blitz, repeating until it's used up and the drink is smooth.

3. Taste and add a little honey, if you'd like it sweeter. Pour into a glass and sprinkle with chopped pistachios to serve.

A Successful Chupe

THE SECRET TO a successful *chupe*, apparently, is a good sprinkling of salty tears. This Chilean seafood casserole is more traditionally topped with cheese and breadcrumbs, then baked to a bubbling golden brown. But the tears add "extra zing" to the dish, and its accompanying salad, when Rosemary breaks down while putting the finishing touches on her dinner party menu.

You can use any seafood in this recipe (in the novel, Rosemary is described as picking apart crabmeat and lobster tails), including leftover cooked fish.

No tears are required, and hopefully there won't be any shed while making or eating this fishy, cheese-topped delight. If you do have a good cry, for any reason, perhaps reduce the stock. And the salt.

Serves 2 to 3 as a main or 4 as a starter

INGREDIENTS

3½ tablespoons (50 grams) butter
4 tablespoons vegetable oil
1 onion, finely chopped
⅔ cup (75 grams) all-purpose flour
2½ cups (600 milliliters) fish stock
1¼ cups (300 milliliters) whole milk
1¼ cups (300 milliliters) white wine
16 ounces (500 grams) cooked seafood (such as a mix of shrimp, dressed crab, and mussels)
Salt and freshly ground black pepper
Pinch of sweet paprika
5 tablespoons breadcrumbs, fresh or dried
¼ cup (50 grams) Parmesan, finely grated

METHOD

1. Place a large pan over medium heat and add the butter and oil, allowing them to melt together before throwing in the onion. Cook, stirring occasionally, for around 5 minutes, or until translucent.

2. Add the flour and continue to cook for 2 minutes, then gradually add the stock, stirring constantly to prevent lumps. Cook for a few more minutes.

3. Add the milk and wine, bring to a simmer, and continue cooking over medium heat for around 10 minutes, or until the sauce thickens. Season to taste with salt, pepper, and paprika.

4. Preheat the oven to 350°F/180°C/160°C fan/gas mark 4. Arrange the seafood on the bottom of a medium-sized casserole dish and top with the sauce.

5. Sprinkle with the breadcrumbs and Parmesan. Bake, uncovered, for around 25 minutes, or until golden and bubbling. Serve with a tear-soaked salad (optional).

10

Food as Fantasy, and Craving Contentment in Angela Carter's "The Bloody Chamber"

IT'S A CASE OF EAT OR BE EATEN IN THIS TERRIFYING BUT RATHER TASTY SHORT STORY.

FOOD IS OFTEN a supporting character in Gothic literature, lurking on a table in the background or being picked at on someone's plate and giving away something that the other characters either haven't noticed or won't admit (or both). In Angela Carter's masterful short story "The Bloody Chamber," food is front and center, both as a physical presence and as a very meaty (and, in one instance, vegetal) metaphor.

The title tale of Carter's 1979 short-story collection takes the French folktale of Bluebeard as its starting point. In *La Barbe bleue*, a late seventeenth-century version written by Charles Perrault, a woman finds her new husband's locked-away secret: a chamber of corpses, each one a former wife.

As always, Carter moves the story along somewhat, shifting the focus to her female protagonist and our narrator, who is never named—perhaps because she represents too many women for her identity to be so defined. If the moral of Perrault's tale is that, for the wife, curiosity leads to peril and punishment, Carter's story exposes the grotesqueness of oppressive male fantasy and marital violence against women.

She also takes the themes of consumption, and being consumed, further, through lavish descriptions of indulgent feasts where the language spills into the sensual and through scenes of sexual desire and entitlement where the language spills into the edible, with an always-present undercurrent of cruelty.

Her Marquis, whose first kiss has "tongue and teeth in it and a rasp of beard," has an insatiable appetite for female flesh. (His title is telling: Carter has spoken and written extensively about Marquis de Sade, a French philosopher who sought to justify his violent sexual crimes against women and children through his writing.)

In "The Bloody Chamber," the Marquis consumes women with the same voraciousness as he devours the decadent meals served at the castle. On their wedding night, she recounts: "He stripped me, gourmand that he was, as if he were stripping the leaves off an artichoke."

It's a terrifying display of power that suggests that he can do whatever he pleases with his new bride. He assesses her with the eye of a connoisseur or like a housewife inspecting a slab of meat. She recalls an etching in which a young girl is manhandled, laid "bare as a lamb chop."

Yet over the course of the story, it becomes clear that our narrator has more agency than the sacrificial lamb she might first appear to be and that this isn't your typical tale of hunter and victim. Perhaps her fate isn't sealed, after all.

Before her husband departs on business, there's the honeymoon dinner, sumptuously described, and perhaps the perfect metaphor for their relationship thus far. An extravagant feast of pheasant with hazelnuts and chocolate is followed by a "white voluptuous cheese," redolent of his generous folds of flesh, and a boozy sorbet made with Asti Spumante and muscat grapes. An "explosion" of champagne is followed by bitter cups of coffee, delicately served in pretty little cups so fragile it's a wonder they don't shatter at the Marquis's touch.

It's a heady meal and as confusing as the narrator's feelings about her husband: she desires him yet is repulsed by him. She has always felt "subtly oppressed" by him.

Fantasies of food reveal her trepidation even as she journeys to the castle. She gazes longingly out of her sleeper carriage window, wearing a nightdress like "heavy water," as houses appear and disappear. Behind those walls and windows, she decides, scenes of domestic contentment are being played out. There's warmth, warm company, and a comforting "supper of sausages" sizzling in a pan—in short, lives that are worlds apart from her fate, where meals are far from humble and the company could better be described as dangerously hot than warm.

Now, alone in the castle, she begins to rebel—and, at first, she does so through food. Coffee and croissants offer some consolation at first, but then she begins to warm to the idea of a solitary meal. Suddenly, she has some agency here. She uses it to gleefully order the type of food a child might request if given the keys to a grand castle: avocado and shrimp ("lots of it"), followed by "every ice-cream in the ice box." Later, she exercises her newfound power and confidence by canceling this "dormitory feast" in favor of sandwiches and coffee in her room.

It harks back to early Gothic literature; around the eighteenth century, appetite and consumption were common themes in texts where female bodies were objectified and consumed, often literally. In the Marquis, and Gothic characters before him, gluttony is pushed to its extreme: cannibalism. Female appetite, however, was taboo. Women didn't devour; they were devoured.

Later in the story, piano tuner Jean-Yves recalls tales of another Marquis, said to have used dogs to hunt young girls "as though they were foxes." Our narrator is not surprised; men still hunt women, she muses—only now potential victims are tracked down in Paris salons and lured into marriage.

Carter takes male oppression, the conspicuous consumption of women, and the taboo of female appetite and weaves them into her story with more than a few twists and turns. Our narrator possesses the power to devour and regain some control, even while her fate remains uncertain right to the end.

Her husband, having unexpectedly returned early from his trip, once again uses the language of eating, this time to express his murderous intentions. He will only, he tells his wife (or "meal"), "grow hungrier" and "more cruel" if she tries to evade him.

Food is a constant in this wicked little tale, from the fancy cakes and box of marrons glacés the Marquis woos the narrator with to the finale, which brings with it the threat of being wholly consumed by her husband and his castle—bringing a frightening meaning to "till death do us part."

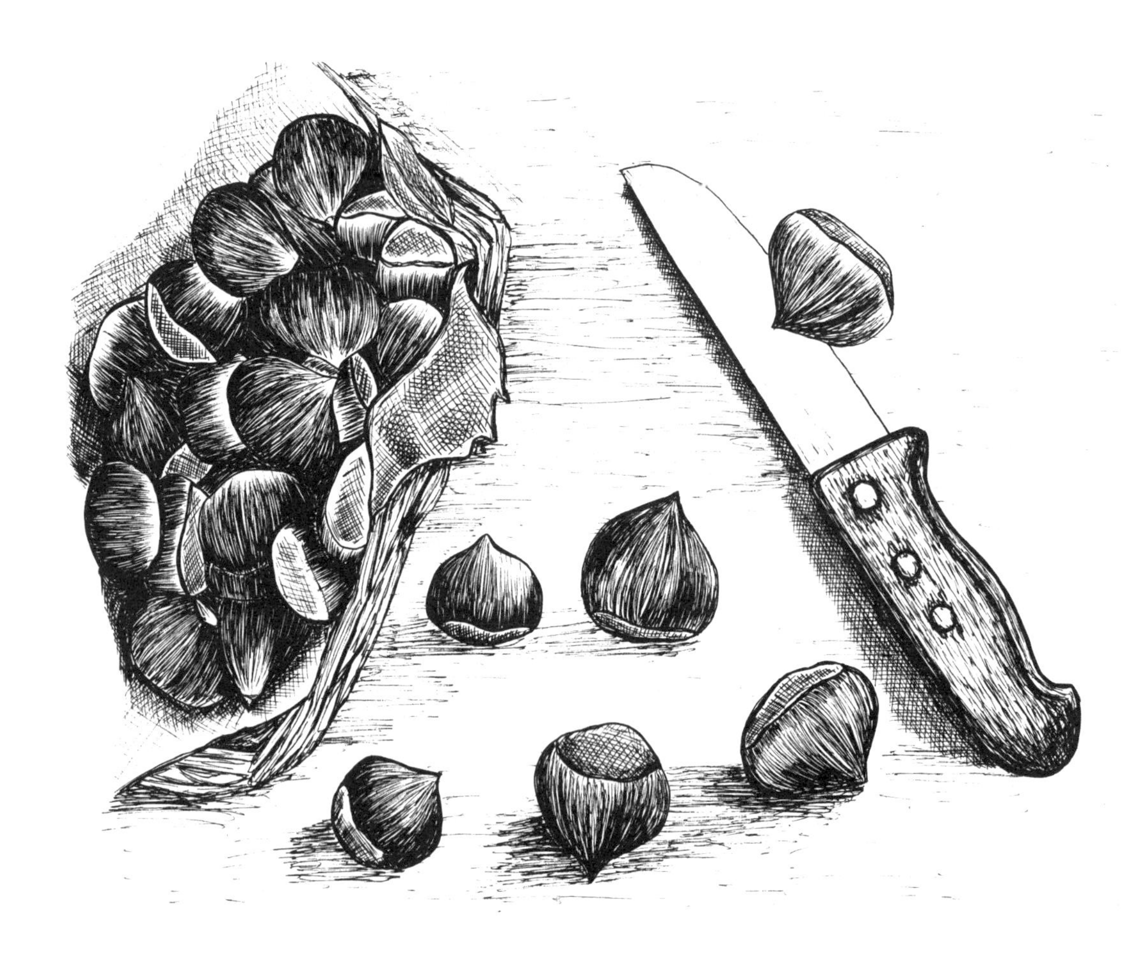

A Box of Marrons Glacés

THE MARQUIS, FLESHY scented with leather and spices, courts our narrator with heavy hands, a soft tread, and surprise gifts, including hothouse flowers and a "box of marrons glacés." These exquisite candied chestnuts, which consume the syrup over several days, take a little patience and more than a little time. But that makes them all the lovelier boxed up as homemade gifts or wedding favors (hopefully for a rather happier couple).

Makes around 36 sweets

INGREDIENTS

3¾ cups (500 grams) fresh chestnuts, still in their shells
1½ cups (300 grams) superfine sugar
1 cup (250 milliliters) water
½ teaspoon vanilla extract, or ½ vanilla pod

METHOD

1. Using a small, sharp knife (or specialist chestnut knife), carefully score a cross on the pointed tip of each chestnut, aiming to cut through only the shell rather than the flesh.

2. Place a medium saucepan of water over high heat and bring to a boil, then add five or six chestnuts at a time, blanching each batch for around 5 minutes.

3. Remove the chestnuts with a slotted spoon and while the next few are simmering away, work quickly to peel away the shell jackets and papery underlayer. This is much easier while they're hot, though you can wear gloves or use a clean tea towel to help rub away the thin skin.

4. To a separate medium pan, add the sugar, water, and vanilla and bring to a boil over a gentle heat, stirring constantly for around 5 minutes, or until all the sugar is dissolved.

5. Add the chestnuts and simmer for around 10 minutes, stirring occasionally. Remove the pan from the heat and cover it, leaving the chestnuts in the syrup for around 24 hours.

6. Around the same time the next day, bring the bathing chestnuts back to a boil over gentle heat and simmer for around 2 to 3 minutes. Remove the pan from the heat and cover it.

7. Repeat the process over the next 3 days, keeping the heat low and not allowing the chestnuts to boil furiously, as overheating the mixture will cause the sugar to crystalize. The chestnuts are ready when they've absorbed most of the liquid and are coated in a sticky, glossy caramel.

8. Allow the chestnuts to cool, then fish them out with a spoon, slanting it to allow any excess syrup to drain off. Line a baking sheet with parchment paper and arrange the chestnuts on top.

9. Preheat the oven to 284°F/140°C/120°C fan/gas mark 1, put the baking sheet in, and then turn off the heat. The chestnuts should dry out within a couple of hours, though you can leave them in a warm, dry place overnight if they need a little more time.

10. Store them in an airtight container or, if these are for gifts, wrap them in cellophane and tie with ribbon—or nestle in pretty little boxes.

A Supper of Sausages

WITH A LONGING heightened by hindsight, the narrator recalls her train journey as she chugs along from the life she knew to another—glamorous yet terrifying—world ruled by the Marquis. The windows they trundle past become, in her mind, "rectangles of domestic lamplight." In one, she fancies, a "supper of sausages" sizzles in a pan, waiting to be served to the stationmaster, whose children are already tucked up in bed.

This imagined moment of domestic contentment is the inspiration for our sausage and cider dish, inspired by a classic French cassoulet. You can make this with any sausages—though nice and fat is best—so it works well as a vegan dish. It's delicious served with roast or mashed potatoes or with some crusty bread to mop up the piquant sauce.

Serves 4

INGREDIENTS

3 tablespoons olive oil, divided
6–8 sausages (approximately 350 grams of sausages), meat or vegetarian
1 medium onion, sliced
4 carrots, sliced into medium rounds
2 tablespoons all-purpose flour
1⅔ cups (400 milliliters) dry cider
¾ cup (200 milliliters) chicken or vegetable stock
2 (14.1-ounce or 400-gram) cans cannellini beans, drained
2 crisp apples (such as Braeburn or similar), cored and cut into wedges
1 tablespoon roughly chopped fresh sage
1 tablespoon roughly chopped fresh thyme
Salt and freshly ground black pepper
1 tablespoon roughly chopped fresh flat-leaf parsley

METHOD

1. Heat 1 tablespoon of the oil in a large casserole pan and add the sausages. Cook them over medium heat for 5 to 6 minutes, until browned on all sides. Remove them from the pan and set them aside.

2. Add the remaining 2 tablespoons oil to the same pan and throw in the onions and carrots. Sweat them, over medium heat, for around 10 minutes, or until soft.

3. Add the flour and stir until it coats the onions and carrots. Cook for a further minute.

4. Turn up the heat, add the cider, and bring to a boil. Reduce the heat and add the stock, beans, apples, sage, and thyme.

5. Slice the sausages diagonally, around 1 centimeter thick. Add them to the pan and season to taste with salt and pepper.

6. Cover the pan and simmer on low for around half an hour, or until all the vegetables are soft and the sauce is thick and rich. If it looks a little watery, continue cooking with the lid off, stirring occasionally until the liquid reduces.

7. To serve, spoon into bowls and sprinkle with parsley.

Chocolate and Hazelnut Mole

A SUMPTUOUS HONEYMOON DINNER has a sinister edge thanks to our narrator's brutish new husband, who shortly afterward abandons her to the lonely castle. The main course is a "Mexican dish of pheasant with hazelnuts and chocolate," which is the inspiration for this velvety chocolate and hazelnut mole sauce. Rich with layers of complex spices, it can be used in a roast pheasant dish, as in the story, or in our jackfruit tacos (both recipes below).

This recipe will yield more sauce than you need for either of those dishes, though you can store the rest in the freezer for up to 2 months.

Makes around 1 liter

INGREDIENTS

2 ripe tomatoes, roughly chopped
1 medium onion, peeled and roughly chopped
1 green pepper, deseeded and roughly chopped
6 cloves garlic, unpeeled
Handful of fresh thyme sprigs
2 tablespoons olive oil, divided
Pinch of salt
8 mild to medium dried chiles (such as mulato, pasilla, or ancho), deseeded
3 tablespoons raisins

6 prunes, roughly chopped
1¼ cups (150 grams) hazelnuts
2 tablespoons pumpkin seeds
½ teaspoon coriander seeds
½ teaspoon cumin seeds
½ teaspoon fennel seeds
6 whole cloves
1 teaspoon ground cinnamon
1 teaspoon ground ginger
2¼ cups (500 milliliters) beef or vegetable stock, divided
5.3 ounces (150 grams) dark chocolate, roughly chopped

METHOD

1. Preheat the oven to 350°F/180°C/160°C fan/gas mark 4. Place the tomatoes, onion, green pepper, garlic, and thyme in a roasting pan, drizzle with 1 tablespoon of the olive oil, and sprinkle with the salt. Roast for 20 to 30 minutes, until charred.

2. Once the garlic is cool enough to handle, squeeze out the flesh and discard the skins, along with the thyme sprigs.

3. Add the remaining 1 tablespoon olive oil to a frying pan over medium heat and add the chiles, raisins, and prunes. Gently fry for 4 to 5 minutes, until the chiles start to release their oil. Remove the contents from the pan and set them aside but keep the oil in the pan.

4. To the same pan, add the hazelnuts and pumpkin seeds and fry over medium heat for a few minutes, tossing the pan to coat them in the chili oil. Continue cooking them for a few more minutes, until lightly browned.

5. Heat a separate small frying pan, with no oil, over medium heat and add the coriander, cumin, and fennel seeds and the cloves. Toast for a few minutes, tossing the pan to prevent them from burning.

6. Remove the pan from the heat and, using a mortar and pestle, grind the seeds to a fine powder.

7. Add the roasted vegetables, garlic, chiles, nuts, powdered spices, cinnamon, and ginger to a food processor (or to a large mixing bowl if using a stick blender). Pour in half the stock (it doesn't matter if it's hot or cold) and blend until smooth.

8. Transfer the mixture to a large saucepan, pressing it through a sieve if you want a smoother texture (use a wooden spoon to push it through).

9. Add the remaining stock, give it a good stir, and warm the mixture over low to medium heat. Once simmering, gradually add the chocolate, stirring as it melts. Taste and add salt if needed.

A Mexican Dish of Pheasant with Hazelnuts and Chocolate

TO RE-CREATE THAT less than romantic first meal at the castle, use our mole recipe to cloak a pheasant before roasting. The result is tender, flavorsome meat with a slightly sticky and richly aromatic sauce.

Browning the bird before roasting prevents the skin from going soggy. This recipe also works with pheasant or chicken thighs or with a whole chicken, browned as described and with the cooking times adjusted accordingly. Whatever you choose, this dish—served with or without the "voluptuous white cheese"—is delicious with roast potatoes, parsnips, and some other veg, like squeaky green beans, to balance the richness of the sauce.

Serves 2

INGREDIENTS

1 medium oven-ready pheasant (around 17.6 ounces or 500 grams)

Salt and freshly ground black pepper

1 tablespoon olive oil

2 tablespoons of butter

2¼ cups (500 milliliters) Chocolate and Hazelnut Mole (page 138)

½ cup (50 grams) crumbly white cheese (optional)

METHOD

1. Preheat the oven to 375°F/190°C/170°C fan/gas mark 5. Season the pheasant well with salt and pepper, rubbing it into the skin.

2. Place the olive oil and butter in a Dutch oven, large casserole dish (big enough to hold the bird), or frying pan over medium heat. Once the butter has melted and it's sizzling a little, place the bird in, skin-side down. Allow it to brown for 2 to 3 minutes, then use large tongs or two wooden spatulas to turn it on one side, again allowing the skin to brown for a couple of minutes. Repeat with the other side.

3. If using a frying pan, transfer the bird to an ovenproof dish or deep-sided baking pan. (If you're using a casserole dish or Dutch oven, it can stay there.)

4. With the bird skin-side up, pour over the mole sauce for an even coating. Cover with a lid or foil and cook for 20 minutes.

5. Uncover and roast for a further 20 minutes. The juices should run clear when the bird is pierced with a skewer or sharp knife; if not, return to the oven and keep checking every 5 minutes or so.

6. Once the bird is cooked through, remove it from the oven, cover it loosely with foil, and allow it to rest for at least 10 minutes before serving. Sprinkle over the white cheese, if using, and carve at the table.

Mole and Jackfruit Tacos

For a vegetarian alternative to the pheasant dish, use the mole for these jackfruit tacos: tasty and more than a little messy.

Serves 4

INGREDIENTS

¾ cup (200 milliliters) red wine vinegar
1 teaspoon superfine sugar
1 teaspoon salt
1 red onion, sliced
¾ cups (200 milliliters) Chocolate and Hazelnut Mole (page 138)
1 (14-ounce or 400-gram) can jackfruit, drained
12 small corn or wheat tortillas
1 medium avocado, peeled and sliced
Handful of fresh cilantro, finely chopped
2 limes, cut into wedges

METHOD

1. Place the vinegar, sugar, salt, and onion in a small saucepan over medium heat.

2. Bring to a boil, then remove the pan from the heat and cover. Leave it to infuse for 10 to 15 minutes, then drain off the liquid and set aside.

3. In a separate medium saucepan, add the mole sauce and jackfruit and stir well to combine. Gently warm over low to medium heat and simmer for a few minutes, adding a splash of water if the mixture looks too thick.

4. Once the jackfruit mixture is warmed through, prepare the tortillas. Place a frying pan over medium heat and add however many tortillas will comfortably fit, heating for a minute on each side. Once done, layer the tortillas between sheets of foil to keep them warm. Repeat until they're all heated through.

5. To serve, place the pickled red onions, jackfruit mixture, avocado, cilantro, and lime wedges in separate serving bowls and arrange them in the middle of the table with the tortillas.

6. To assemble each taco, place a generous spoonful of the jackfruit on a tortilla, top with avocado, onions, a sprinkling of cilantro, and a squeeze of lime, and fold to eat.

Sorbet of Muscat Grapes and Asti Spumante

THE PERFECT END to a sumptuous yet sinister honeymoon meal, a sorbet of muscat grapes and Asti Spumante is an odd blend of the sophisticated and the childlike. Perhaps it represents still-innocent tastes aiming for sophistication, or perhaps it's more of a reflection on the Marquis: he has money but isn't exactly what you'd call classy.

Having said that, there is something quite charming about this sorbet: refreshing with a discernible sweetness from the Asti sparkling wine and with a warmth of alcohol that makes it decidedly grown-up.

If you can find muscat grapes, do use them—though any white (eating) grapes will do. You can also substitute champagne or any other sparkling wine for the Spumante, though bear in mind it won't be so sweet. Whether this is a good thing depends on your taste buds, so adjust the sugar levels if needed.

Serves 4

INGREDIENTS

2¾ cups (500 grams) white grapes, picked through and washed
¼ cup (50 grams) granulated sugar
Pinch of salt
½ cup (125 milliliters) Asti Spumante

METHOD

1. Place the grapes in a food processor and blitz for just a few seconds, to release the liquid without fully blending them.

2. Place a sieve over a bowl and pour in the grape mixture, pressing with a spoon or rubber spatula until you've squeezed out most of the juice.

3. Transfer the juice to a small saucepan and, over low heat, whisk in the sugar and salt before adding the fizz.

4. Continue to whisk for a minute, then switch to a wooden spoon, stirring until the sugar has dissolved (this should just take a few minutes). Set aside to cool.

5. Once it's at room temperature, transfer the mixture to a tub with a lid and place in the fridge for 1 to 2 hours, until chilled.

6. If you have an ice cream maker, churn as per instructions until it reaches the desired texture (like snow), then freeze for at least 3 hours before serving. If not, place the tub in the freezer and freeze for around 4 hours, removing every 45 minutes to give it a good stir/whisk with a fork.

7. Remove the sorbet from the freezer 10 to 15 minutes before serving, to soften.

Avocado and Shrimp, Lots of It

ABANDONED BY (OR temporarily liberated from) her husband and all alone in the coldly vast castle, our heroine faces daily life with a child-like imagination and whimsy. Wondering what she should request for dinner, she ponders a "fowl in cream" or a festive "varnished turkey."

Eventually, she lands on avocado and shrimp—"lots of it." This, and going against convention by having "no entrée at all" and instead skipping straight to "every ice-cream in the ice box," seems like a rebellion against the prison she has walked right into.

This recipe serves four people as a starter and can be easily scaled up or down—so you can make lots of it and devour every creamy, spicy mouthful, if you like.

Serves 4

INGREDIENTS

Chili Sauce

4 dehydrated chiles

2 cloves garlic, crushed

¾ teaspoon superfine sugar

1½ tablespoons white wine vinegar

Salt and freshly ground black pepper

2 large ripe avocados

2 cups (200 grams) shrimp, cooked and peeled

Marie Rose Sauce

½ cup (120 milliliters) mayonnaise
2 tablespoons ketchup
Juice of ½ lemon
Salt and freshly ground black pepper

METHOD

1. First, make the chili sauce. Boil a small pot of water. Place the chiles in a small heatproof bowl and cover them with the just-boiled water. Allow them to soak for 10 minutes, then remove them from the bowl.

2. Transfer the chiles to a food processor along with the other sauce ingredients and blitz until smooth (you could also use a large bowl and handheld stick blender), then pour into a small saucepan and simmer over low heat for around 10 minutes. Set the chili sauce aside to cool while you prepare the rest of the dish.

3. Halve and stone the avocados. Scoop out the flesh (leaving a fine layer and taking care not to break the shell) and dice it to form small cubes.

4. To make the Marie Rose sauce, combine the mayonnaise, ketchup, and lemon juice in a large bowl and mix well. Season with salt and pepper.

5. Add the diced avocado flesh and shrimp to the Marie Rose sauce, stirring so they're well coated.

6. Spoon the mixture back into the avocado shells and drizzle over the cooled chili sauce to serve.

11

Clinging on to Comfort Food with Cold, Dead Hands in Susan Hill's *The Woman in Black*

FOOD BEGINS TO LEAVE A BAD TASTE IN THE MOUTH, AND A CHILL IN THE SOUL, IN THIS TERRIFYING GHOST STORY.

IT'S NORMAL TO remember a really good meal. At first, though, it seems a little odd that Arthur Kipps, our reluctant narrator, would so fondly remember a simple supper enjoyed just before his life was upturned by a malicious, vengeful ghost. Surely enough has happened since to render one pub meal, however delicious, incidental?

Perhaps it's precisely because of what happened afterward that he so desperately clings to the memory of this last supper: a glass of mulled wine by a roaring, open fire; a mouthwatering meal of "home-made broth, sirloin of beef, apple and raisin tart with cream, and some Stilton cheese"; and half a bottle of claret. The murmur of chatter reverberates through the walls from the public bar, adding to the sense of normality and warmth that characterizes this scene. Instead of distracting from the insidious tension, from the menace that lurks in the flickering shadows, and from the cloak of tragedy that the present-day Arthur—the one telling this story—can't shrug off, it serves as a stark contrast that highlights them all the more.

Food, with its inherent nurturing and comforting qualities and, conversely, its ability to be weaponized or used as a trap, is key here, helping to tell Arthur's sad tale in the most subtle and Gothic of ways.

There even appears to be a nod, or perhaps a hark back, to another newly qualified solicitor of the Gothic canon: Jonathan Harker. Occupation aside, they are both (so early in their careers) sent off on seemingly simple missions that involve eccentric and rather creepy characters and mortal danger. They also both love food—at least, before events get a little out of hand and evil takes the reins.

In a detail that recalls Jonathan's note to "get recipe for Mina" in *Dracula*, Arthur writes a little note to his fiancée, Stella, while waiting for his supper. He imagines their future, where they might live after being married, and how his career might progress. Given that we have already met Arthur's wife, Esmé, at the start of the novel, before our narrator is dragged back to a memory so terrible he has attempted to bury it in the dark depths of his mind, we can assume that things don't end so well for Arthur and Stella.

Back at the Gifford Arms, our young solicitor rests that night with a full stomach, a sense of well-being and contentment, and a pleasantly fuzzy head (thanks to the wine). And he wakes to an imminent nightmare. This recollection is of much more than a comforting pub meal, albeit a very good one. It's swaddled in the memory of the last time Arthur was truly, or even just a little bit, content. What follows is the unraveling of this comfort, beginning with momentary stabs of uneasiness and escalating to pure terror.

Those comforting pub kitchen scents of roast meat, mulling spices, and baking pies drift away, along with the sounds of convivial chatter. In their place creep in dank, chilly air, the cold stares of strangers, and bad omens that would spoil anyone's appetite.

The novel opens with a festive scene tinged with sadness. The air is scented with the aromas of wood smoke and clove-studded oranges, while a gloriously Gothic tower of gilded fruit decorates the room. Around him, Arthur's family is excited about Christmas and all it promises, yet he cannot quite muster the enthusiasm to enjoy the feast, and the ghost stories the children revel in only make him shudder.

The would-be soothing scents and sounds of nature mingle with less auspicious signs: leaf mold, the cries of nocturnal wildlife, a chilling dampness that lingers in the air. If Arthur seems unable to fully enjoy a meal, with even a glass of malt whiskey "beside the crackling fire" failing to comfort him, what comes next (or, in the chronology of his lifetime, has come before) explains why. Hill weaves in subtle clues to both his state of mind and the nature of previous events. His lack of appetite, for food and festivities, is part of that.

So, too, is the house he and his family now call home. Arthur's sense of déjà vu when he first sees Monk's Piece, somehow knowing he will one day call it his own, introduces more than a touch of the uncanny to the proceedings. As he looks back to his first encounter with another equally fateful house, Eel Marsh, we become increasingly aware that the domestic abode and its promises of coziness and contentment are not to be trusted.

There are clues, too, as he is dragged back to his most feared memories. Now, recounting his story with the terrible knowledge of what happens next, he lingers on details that are simultaneously comforting and portentous. Before departing for the market town of Crythin Gifford, on an ill-fated mission to attend the funeral of Alice Drablow, the sole occupant of Eel Marsh House, and see to her last will and testament, he catches a waft of roast chestnuts. Yet his description of the chestnut sellers and their "red-hot pools of light" shifts this away from cozy and cheering to dangerous and verging on the diabolical.

Still, his life is in "apple-pie order" when he arrives at the Gifford Arms, and he is given the warmest of welcomes with his hot meal. He also enjoys a hearty breakfast the next morning and now flinches at the memory of how contentedly he slept, how eagerly he sprang from his bed to face the day.

The pub kitchen once again releases aromas of bread, pies, and cakes, as the town prepares for market day. Arthur, however, feels "like a spectre at some cheerful feast," dressed as he is in mourning garb for the funeral. The description echoes his feelings at the start of the novel, suggesting that this becomes his default mood. It's also, again, portentous, coming so soon before he first sets eyes upon the woman in black.

Arthur does partake in the "excellent lunch" later on, though it all starts to feel a bit queasy; a dizzying array of tureens of soup, heaps of vegetables, and platters of meat is accompanied by talk of the Eel Marsh House ghost.

Once at the house, standing in creepy quietude at the end of a mist-shrouded causeway and appearing the very embodiment of purgatory, Arthur finds that his appetite fades. He takes a walk to work up an appetite yet can only sip a dusty old brandy. He's able to eat again only when back at the hotel and later accepts Mr. Daily's dinner invitation—a thinly veiled attempt to take Arthur away from Mrs. Drablow's house and her affairs—to feast on roast pheasant and "a huge treacle tart."

The contrast between his mood at Eel Marsh House—which he has visited despite various villagers' refusal to go anywhere near it—and away from its ghastly gates is reflected in his appetite. Determined to complete the task set by his boss in London, to search for Mrs. Drablow's private papers so they can get her affairs in order, Arthur refuses to be scared away from the house. As the ghost's grip on his psyche squeezes tighter, however, he loses the will to eat (and to live) altogether. His attempts to bring some warmth to the late widow's house, bringing in hampers of provisions and busying himself with cheering up the "gloomy kitchen," fall flat, to say the least.

The most he manages to eat is a "limited but not unpleasant supper," shared with the dog, Spider (who, by this point, is the fine line between Arthur and crushing loneliness, or even madness).

Toward the end, Arthur struggles to drag himself to the breakfast table. Dining alone, at first a pleasure, has become unbearably poignant. He cannot face food and drinks only tea.

The woman in black, whom he at one point fancies is someone in the house who wakes in the night, searching for food and drink, is something altogether more sinister: a haunted ghost, ravenous for revenge.

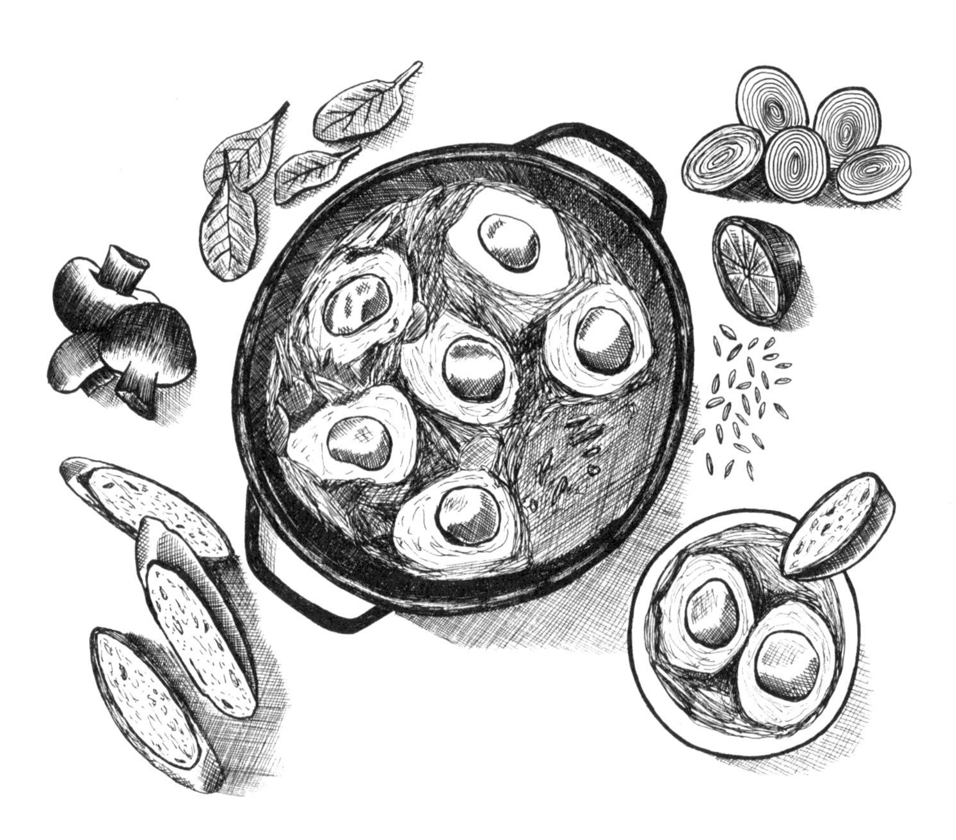

Baked Eggs and Cream

Early on, food is framed as a cure for ill health and troubled minds, as Mr. Bentley suggests that Arthur fill himself up "with fresh air and good eggs and cream." We later learn that Arthur armed himself with food as a way to stave off the damp and decidedly undomestic air of Eel Marsh House.

It doesn't really work out, of course, though a portion of this rich and particularly satisfying breakfast or brunch (or anytime) dish may have provided a morsel of comfort.

This recipe yields enough for a hearty portion for four people, or it can serve eight as part of a bigger breakfast spread. You can also adjust the number of eggs accordingly—you won't regret having extra of the wonderful creamy sauce, which is delicious spooned on toast or (if you have some left in the dish after dishing out the eggs) even tossed through pasta.

Serves 4 as a main or up to 8 as a side dish

INGREDIENTS

3 tablespoons olive oil

3¾ cups (250 grams) chestnut mushrooms, cleaned and thinly sliced

1 large leek, trimmed, halved, and thinly sliced

13⅓ cups (400 grams) fresh spinach

1 tablespoon fennel seeds

1 tablespoon dried tarragon

2 teaspoons Dijon mustard

Juice of ½ lemon

1¼ cups (300 milliliters) heavy cream

⅔ cup (75 grams) cheddar, divided

Salt and freshly ground black pepper

8 medium eggs

METHOD

1. Place the oil in a large ovenproof Dutch oven or casserole dish. Once heated, add the mushrooms and gently fry them over medium heat for 5 to 6 minutes, until they start to release their water and get a little color.

2. Add the leeks and sauté for around 5 minutes, to soften, then add the spinach and stir until it begins to wilt (this should take only a minute or so).

3. Add the fennel seeds, tarragon, mustard, and lemon juice and stir well.

4. Add the cream and half of the cheddar. Stir until the cheese has melted and everything is nicely combined.

5. Season with a good pinch of salt and pepper and remove the pan from the heat.

6. Preheat the oven to 390°F/200°C/180°C fan/gas mark 6. Use a spoon to make eight wells in the sauce, then gently crack an egg into each.

7. Sprinkle the remaining cheese over the eggs and transfer the pan to the oven, baking for around 20 minutes, or until the white parts of the egg are opaque and the yolks still have a little wobble.

Mulled Wine

A HEARTY, COCKLE-WARMING MEAL often comes before the horror and the haunting, and Arthur's starts with a suitably comforting glass of mulled wine, recommended by the Gifford Arms' landlord and sipped by the fire while the "murmur of voices" from the bar provides background noise.

One or two glasses of this will leave you in a "warm glow of well-being and contentment," too, and hopefully the days that follow won't disturb that feeling.

Serves 4 to 6

INGREDIENTS

1 orange

1 tablespoon cloves

Slightly over 3 cups (750 milliliters) full-bodied red wine

4 tablespoons superfine sugar

1 cinnamon stick

1 star anise

Peel of 1 lemon

Peel of 1 orange

3 tablespoons brandy (optional)

Cinnamon sticks, star anise, and slices of orange, to garnish

METHOD

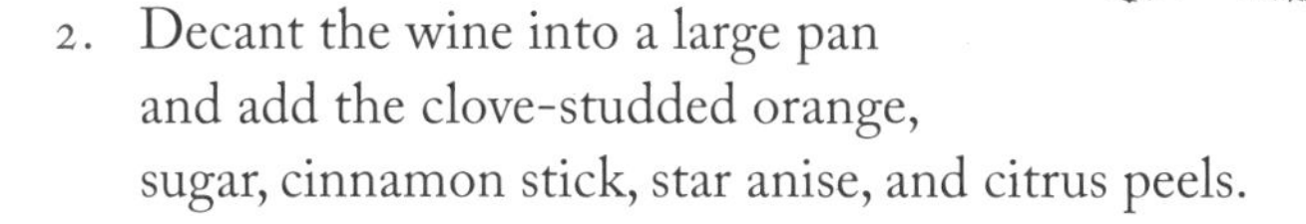

1. Stud the orange with the cloves and set it aside.

2. Decant the wine into a large pan and add the clove-studded orange, sugar, cinnamon stick, star anise, and citrus peels.

3. Heat on low for 10 to 15 minutes, stirring occasionally, until the sugar is dissolved (take care not to bring to a boil).

4. Remove the pan from the heat, cover it, and leave the mixture to infuse for at least half an hour.

5. For a smoother mulled wine, without "bits," pour it into another pan through a sieve. You can also leave the aromatics in, as they'll continue to infuse the wine with warming spices.

6. To serve, gently heat the wine and stir in the brandy, if using. Pour it into mugs or heatproof glasses and garnish.

Bone Broth

A "HOME-MADE BROTH" IS the opener of Arthur's memorable meal. Nourishing and comforting, it also has a subtle creepiness and savagery: it is, after all, a bowlful of boiled bones (or the essence of them).

Bone broth seems especially apt for this pub meal scene, reflecting its dramatic irony and sense of impending doom.

Serves 4

INGREDIENTS

1 kilogram (about 35 ounces) beef bones, preferably a mix of marrow bones and bones with a little meat on them (such as oxtail, short ribs, or knuckle bones)

3 large carrots, roughly chopped

2 onions, peeled and quartered

1 bulb garlic, broken into cloves but unpeeled

8½ cups (2 liters) water

2 celery stalks, roughly chopped

2 bay leaves

2 tablespoons black peppercorns

1 tablespoon cider vinegar

METHOD

1. Preheat the oven to 390°F/200°C/180°C fan/gas mark 6. Place the bones, carrots, onions, and garlic in a deep roasting pan or baking dish and roast for 20 minutes. Toss the contents of the pan and continue to roast for around 20 minutes more, or until deeply browned.

2. Meanwhile, add the water to a large casserole dish or saucepan and throw in the celery, bay leaves, peppercorns, and vinegar. Add the roasted bones and vegetables, being sure to tip in any juices. Add more water, if needed, so everything is just covered.

3. Over medium heat, bring to a boil, then reduce to the lowest heat, partially cover (leaving the lid slightly askew), and simmer gently for at least 8 hours, removing the lid every so often to skim off any foam and excess fat. (Note: You can simmer at intervals, removing the pot from the heat and continuing later on or even the following day. Alternatively, you can cook the broth in a slow cooker on low for the same amount of time.)

4. The longer you allow the broth to simmer away, the more packed with flavor it will be. Add more water, if necessary, to ensure that the bones and vegetables remain fully submerged.

5. Remove the pot from the heat and allow the broth to cool slightly, so it's just warm. Strain through a fine-meshed sieve and discard the bones and vegetables. Once fully cooled, decant the broth into sealable containers and store overnight in the fridge.

6. A solid white lid of fat will form on top of each—remove this and discard before warming the broth to serve.

Potted Sirloin of Beef

AFTER THE BONE broth comes the sirloin of beef, a pub classic that screams of comfort. Later, of course, the only screams are induced by horror.

This recipe is inspired by Arthur's meal and also Hannah Glasse's recipe To Pot Beef Like Venison, which involves salting beef and letting it "lye" for several days, turning twice a day. This is a little simpler (and quicker, requiring a mere 5 hours in the fridge and 3 hours' cooking time) but yields similar results: meat that's tender and soft as butter.

It can be portioned and served warm (it's especially good with mashed potatoes) or, continuing the recipe from step 4, potted in a more traditional sense, for a coarse, flavor-packed pâté.

Serves 2

INGREDIENTS

15.8 ounces (450 grams) rolled joint of sirloin
1 tablespoon salt
2 cups (500 milliliters) water
1 teaspoon black peppercorns
2 bay leaves
3½ tablespoons (50 grams) butter, softened (if serving as a pâté), plus 2 tablespoons (25 grams), melted, if storing
Salt and freshly ground black pepper

METHOD

1. Rub the beef joint with the salt, place it in a bowl, cover it, and keep it in the fridge for around 5 hours or overnight.

2. Preheat the oven to 320°F/160°C/140°C fan/gas mark 3. Place the salted beef in a casserole dish and cover it with the water, adding more if needed, so it's submerged. Add the peppercorns and bay leaves and bake, covered with a lid, for around 3 hours, or until the meat is tender enough to easily break up with a fork.

3. Remove the dish from the oven and, if serving as a meal, transfer the joint to a cutting board and carve thick slices (or simply halve, for two tender hunks of beef). Reserve any juices. Serve with vegetables, roast or mashed potatoes, and some of the juices spooned over.

4. To make a coarse pâté, allow the beef to cool before transferring it to a large bowl. Reserve any juices. Use a fork to flake up the meat, then add the butter and around 2 tablespoons of the pan juices.

5. Continue to mix with the fork, gradually adding more of the juices, until it's well combined and at your desired texture (somewhere between spoonable and spreadable is ideal). Taste and season with salt and pepper as needed.

6. For a smoother texture, after step 4, transfer a little at a time to a mortar and pestle and grind to a paste, adding juices as you go. Have a jar or bowl ready for the finished pâté so you can set it aside as you go.

7. To store, pack the meat into a large jar and top with the melted butter, which will form a cap when refrigerated. The pâté will keep well in the fridge for a few days, ready to be spread on toast, served with crackers, or taken out on a picnic.

Apple and Raisin Tart

BEFORE THE TERROR came the tart. . . . This apple and raisin tart punctuates what seems to be the last meal Arthur actually enjoys. Served with a dollop of cream and some Stilton cheese, it's a suitably bittersweet pause before his world is destroyed by a vengeful ghost.

Our recipe has a layer of apple purée and raisins below the apple slices to create a sticky, almost caramel sweetness.

Serves 6 to 8

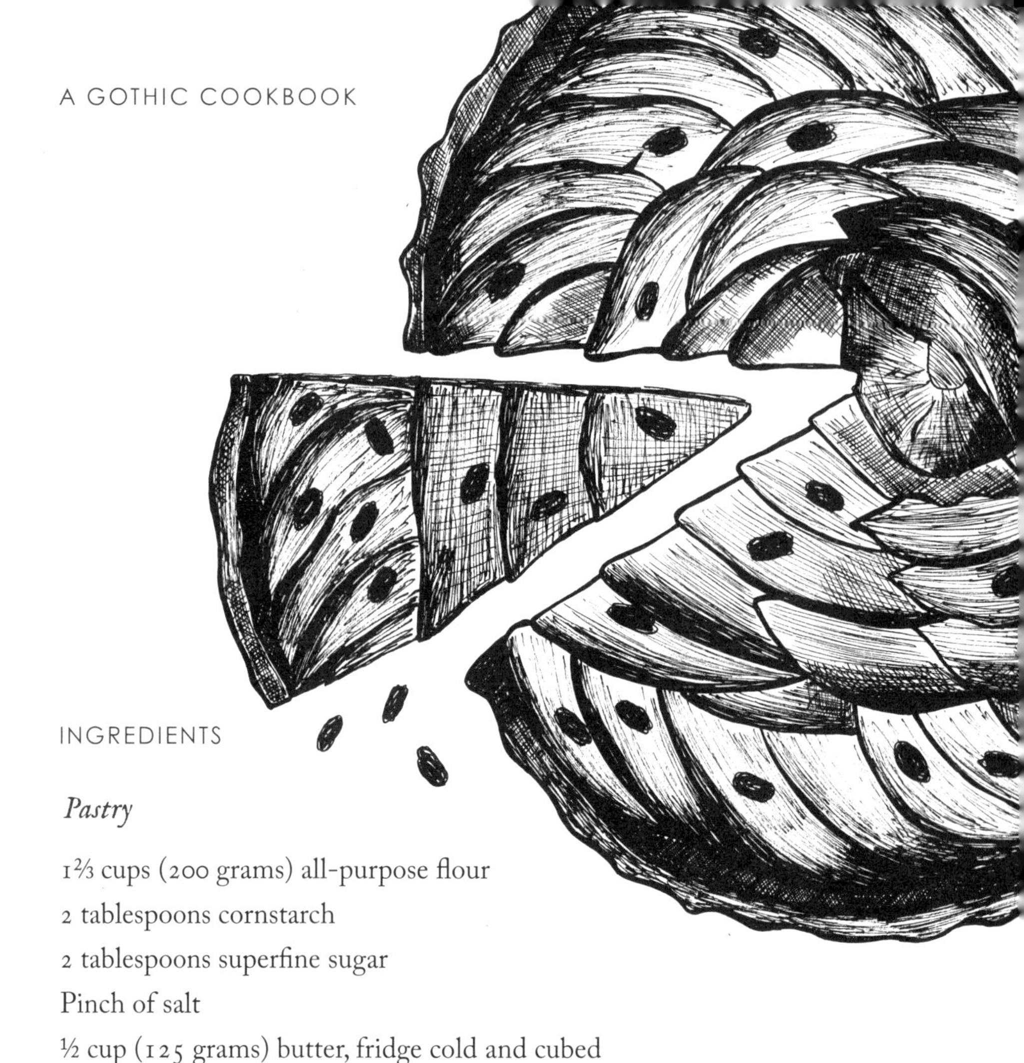

INGREDIENTS

Pastry

1⅔ cups (200 grams) all-purpose flour

2 tablespoons cornstarch

2 tablespoons superfine sugar

Pinch of salt

½ cup (125 grams) butter, fridge cold and cubed

1 egg, beaten

3 tablespoons cold water

Filling

4½ cups (800 grams) apples, divided

5 tablespoons golden caster sugar, divided

1 teaspoon cinnamon

2 tablespoons water

Juice of ½ lemon

4 tablespoons raisins, divided

1 tablespoon apricot jam

Softly whipped cream, for serving

METHOD

1. Preheat the oven to 350°F/180°C/160°C fan/gas mark 4. Butter a 9-inch (23-centimeter) round, loose-bottomed tart pan.

2. To make the pastry, sieve the flour, cornstarch, and sugar together into a large mixing bowl and add the salt. Rub the butter into the dry ingredients with your fingertips until you achieve a texture like rough breadcrumbs.

3. Make a well in the center and add the egg along with a little of the water. Using your hand or a spatula, gradually incorporate with the dry ingredients while adding the water a trickle at a time, until it forms a firm dough.

4. Wrap the dough in plastic wrap and refrigerate for half an hour. Flour a surface, then roll it out thinly so it's large enough to slightly overhang the pan. Use the dough to line the pan, allowing it to spill over the sides. Prick the base a few times with a fork, then cover it with parchment paper and fill with ceramic baking beans or dried pulse.

5. Bake for around 20 minutes. Set the pastry case aside to cool.

6. Meanwhile, to make the filling, peel, core, and roughly chop a third of the apples and add them to a medium saucepan with 3 tablespoons of the sugar and the cinnamon and the water. Heat on low, stirring occasionally, for 10 to 15 minutes—depending on the variety of apple—until very soft. Set aside.

7. Peel, core, quarter, and thinly slice the remaining apples and toss them with the lemon juice and the remaining 2 tablespoons sugar.

8. Assemble the tart by first spooning the purée into the pastry case. Top with 3 tablespoons of the raisins and then the apple slices, starting at the outer edge and layering toward the center in a spiral. Repeat to use up all the slices—they should completely fill the pastry case. Scatter over the remaining 1 tablespoon raisins.

9. Warm the jam in a small saucepan over low heat, then spoon it over the apples, using a pastry brush so it covers evenly. Bake the tart for around 20 minutes, or until the pastry is golden and the apples are soft. Slice and serve warm with a dollop of whipped cream.

12

A Ravenous Ghost and Sweet Things in Toni Morrison's *Beloved*

IN MORRISON'S SEMINAL GHOST STORY, FOOD AND HUNGER HIGHLIGHT THE BARBARISM OF SLAVERY AND HOW IT SEVERS THE STRONGEST OF BONDS.

FOOD IS LIFE. Food is love. Food is how we show love and how we keep those we love alive. This is as it should be for the characters in *Beloved*. But it isn't their reality. The abhorrence of slavery has robbed them of the ability to meet these essential human needs and desires. Their emptiness can never be filled. Their hunger can never be sated.

That hunger, on both a basic physical level and a far deeper emotional level, haunts every page of the novel. Food appears as the disjointed crumbs of memory, as a presence during a nightmarish scene, and as a symbol of something warm and comforting that remains torturously out of grasp. It's an escape that's impossible and a distraction from horrors that are equally impossible to truly ignore or banish.

A nourishing force becomes tangled and mangled, reflecting the fact that, under the unnatural, brutal condition of slavery, the most powerful of human instincts are suppressed, subverted, and even severed.

Kneading dough for bread is an act of "beating back the past." Sethe's mother-in-law, Baby Suggs, has lost so much—and so many—in her lifetime that she barely allows herself to remember one baby girl, recalling only that she "loved the burned bottom of bread." Later, Baby Suggs herself dies "soft as cream." And then there's the eponymous Beloved, with her insatiable, and at times sinister, appetite for "sweet things."

Her twin desires for sugar and Sethe's love reflect a common theme that ties all of the seemingly disparate characters together: a longing for something to fill the void and the tragic reality that nothing truly can.

As the story opens, Sethe and her daughter Denver are living in apparent freedom in a house referred to only as 124. Food is littered through the scene. Food is how the ghost, who haunts the home with "a baby's venom," announces itself, chasing away family members one by one.

Kettles full of hot chickpeas overturned and spilled on the floor, a baby's handprints appearing in a cake, and a trail of soda cracker crumbs by the door are more than enough to send Sethe's two sons running from the "lively spite" that fills the house. What should be the comforting chaos of a family house is upturned, like steaming pots from a stove. Nourishment is weaponized by a ravenous presence.

From the first pages, the ghost joins the family through food. Rather than being part of a convivial gathering around the dinner table, though, her interactions border on the aggressive. It sets the scene for a tale in which nurture, often symbolized by food, is subverted and hungry hearts and stomachs are never quite filled.

Beloved, having emerged from the stream, embodies this. She is, from the beginning, a bottomless pit of longing. She consumes "cup after cup of water," perhaps a metaphor for the absence of her mother's milk. As time passes, she appears to grow "plumper" and taller while Sethe seems to shrink. Yet nothing Beloved eats will be enough to sate her emotional hunger, and no amount of water will quench her thirst for Sethe, who is "licked, tasted, eaten" by Beloved's eyes.

Denver, too, seeks solace in food. Abandoned by her brothers and with her grandmother dead, she feels her mother slipping away. Then Paul D—"the last of the Sweet Home men"—arrives and seems to exorcise the ghost, "the only other company she had."

She stuffs food into the void, salvaging burned biscuits and a jar of jam from the wreckage and cobbling together a "meal" on a broken shard of plate. Like the other food Morrison describes throughout the novel, it doesn't quite do its job. She eats it miserably, failing to quieten her loneliness.

That she chooses to eat on the porch, rather than in the kitchen, seems significant. Denver removes herself from the family, or the crumbs of it, perhaps because she can't bear to spend time in what should be the heart of the home.

It once was just that, if only for a short time. The abundance described when Sethe arrives at 124, babe in arms, is biblical. The feast multiplies, with two hens becoming five turkeys and three or four pies growing to "ten (maybe twelve)." The house is loud with laughter and warmth, and even Baby Suggs's generosity and kindness spark jealousy and suspicion from neighbors. The gaiety doesn't—can't—last in a world where Sethe can be only a slave or a fugitive.

Still, she often occupies herself by cooking, kneading bread, and tending to simmering pots of stew and rutabaga (swede) for guests who never come and a ghost who is more likely to upend the pans than eat what's prepared in them. Sethe's busyness seems, as at the plantation, to be a futile attempt to beat back the past.

Back there, at the ironically named Sweet Home, food is enjoyed only when it represents tiny rebellions, snatched moments that feel like shadows of freedom. Sixo obsesses over achieving the perfect "night-cooked potatoes," burying them in a hole with hot rocks. The result is reliably bad, whether raw or shriveled, but the enslaved men relish those moments.

Those feelings are clearer still in the description of them enjoying a "feast of new corn," stolen from the crops. The juice and flavor are described as "jailed," quick to run free when allowed. The silk, which binds it and keeps it captive, is "fine and loose and free." The metaphor is layered, with strong sexual overtones, and the scene is both underpinned and overshadowed by the fact that the people in the scene are not free. Even the "simple joy" of eating must be surreptitious.

Like the myrtle Sethe props in the corner of a white woman's kitchen, attempting to grasp some sense of home, that freedom is never allowed to be real, even after she has physically escaped. Sethe can never fully shake off the shackles and scars of Sweet Home, and Beloved is a manifestation of that: a physical reminder of a brutal fate truly worse than death and the consequence of a motherly bond severed.

At Sweet Home, Sethe's body is not her own. Neither are her children nor her husband. As Morrison writes in a foreword to her novel, Black women were *required* to have babies but were never *allowed* to be mothers.

The plantation's name is suggestive of a driving force behind slavery: the demand for sugar and the greed of those profiting from it.

Bittersweetness is woven through Morrison's narrative like spun sugar. On a more joyous occasion than her solitary jam and burned biscuits on the porch, Denver devours licorice, horehound (old-fashioned boiled sweets, or "cough candy"), peppermint, and lemonade at a fair, and it buoys her. In a similar way to Beloved, who arrives shortly after this scene, she is "soothed by sugar."

Both have a bottomless hunger for Sethe, whose motherly instinct, though deeply scarred, still strives to feed them. That emotional hunger emerges as a physical hunger, primarily for sweets.

From the moment Denver offers Beloved sweet bread, "sugar could always be counted on to please her." She greedily devours any edible (and borderline inedible) saccharine substances, from beeswax and sugar sandwiches to molasses that's turned "hard and brutal in the can."

As Morrison writes: "It was as if sweet things were what she was born for." That single, deceptively simple phrase encapsulates the deep, cloying need that emanates from Beloved, provides a chilling reminder that she can never reach her potential, and reminds us of the fate her mother so brutally liberated her from.

Peppermint Creams

Spite, disapproval, and overt racism can't prevent Sethe, Paul D, and Denver from having a grand time when the carnival's in town. Denver buys horehound sweets, licorice, lemonade, and peppermint. Together with the sights and sounds of the carnival, and the community spirit of the crowd, they make her giddy with delight. For one evening, Denver feels normal, even happy.

When you need to be "soothed by sugar," these simple yet wonderfully sweet and refreshing peppermint creams are the perfect solution. They're especially lovely dipped in dark chocolate, providing a contrast in texture and adding an earthy, rich sweetness.

Makes 20–25

INGREDIENTS

1 egg white
2⅓ cups (300 grams) powdered sugar, sieved, divided, plus extra for dusting
2–3 drops peppermint extract
½ cup (100 grams) dark chocolate, broken into small pieces (optional)

METHOD

1. Lightly whisk the egg white, by hand in a small bowl or in a stand mixer, until it's just starting to foam (but far from forming peaks).

2. Add around a third of the powdered sugar, beating well with a wooden spoon as you do, and then drop in the peppermint, mixing well.

3. Gradually add the remaining powdered sugar, continuing to beat the dough and swapping to your hands when it becomes too stiff for a spoon.

4. Dust a surface with powdered sugar and knead the dough until smooth. Dust with more powdered sugar and roll out to a thickness of around ½ centimeter.

5. Line a large baking sheet with parchment paper and dust it with powdered sugar. Stamp out rounds from the dough using a small cutter (around 3 centimeters), placing the peppermint creams on the baking sheet as you go. Keep gathering up the scraps and roll out and stamp again until most of the dough is used up.

6. Cover the creams loosely with another sheet of parchment paper and set aside to dry for 2 to 3 hours, until they are no longer sticky to the touch.

7. Bring a small pan of water to a simmer. Melt the chocolate, if using a small heatproof bowl set over the pan, stirring until silky. Or you can place the chocolate in a small microwavable bowl and heat it on full power for 20 seconds at a time, stirring and repeating until fully melted.

8. Allow the chocolate to cool for just a couple of minutes, then carefully dip each peppermint cream into it, coating half. Place the candies back on the parchment paper and leave them to set for another 2 to 3 hours or overnight. Store them in an airtight container and eat within a month.

Brown Butter-Sugar Sand Cookies

DENVER OBSERVES THE connection between Beloved and sweet things, disappointed by her failed attempts to form a real bond with Beloved, who "only has eyes for Sethe"; she describes the mysterious guest's breath as "sugary from fingerfuls of molasses or sand-cookie crumbs."

There are various theories about the origins of sand cookies and whether German or Dutch colonizer settlers introduced them to America. Wherever they came from, these crumbly, shortbread-like cookies—named for their texture—remain a popular treat and are sometimes decorated with red and green icing for Christmas.

For our recipe, we're browning the butter before making the dough, imbuing the sand cookies with a caramel nuttiness and a subtle, fudge-like layer.

Makes around 24 cookies

INGREDIENTS

¾ cup (175 grams) butter

¾ cup (150 grams) superfine sugar

1 teaspoon vanilla extract or paste

½ teaspoon baking powder

1⅔ cups (200 grams) all-purpose flour

Flaky sea salt

METHOD

1. Place the butter in a small saucepan over low to medium heat, stirring until melted and then allowing to brown, shaking the pan occasionally for 10 to 15 minutes. It's ready when it's a nutty color and just on the edge of burned.

2. Transfer the butter to a medium mixing bowl or stand mixer and allow it to cool at room temperature for around an hour, so it's solidified but soft.

3. Then give it a whisk with a fork, add the sugar and vanilla, and beat until fluffy, using a wooden spoon or the beater attachment on a stand mixer.

4. In a small bowl mix the baking powder into the flour, then slowly add to the butter mixture, beating as you go, to form a smooth dough.

5. Flour a surface and tip out the dough. Knead it a little, then form it into two to three sausages, roughly the diameter of a rolling pin. Wrap these in plastic wrap and chill them for an hour in the fridge.

6. Preheat the oven to 350°F/180°C/160°C fan/gas mark 4. Line two baking sheets with parchment paper and brush with a little oil.

7. Remove the logs from the fridge and slice them to form cookies around ½ centimeter thick. Arrange the cookies on the prepared sheets, spacing them out well, as they may spread just a little when baking. (You might need a third baking sheet, depending on the size of your cookies.)

8. Sprinkle them with a little sea salt and bake them for 18 to 20 minutes, until just kissed with gold. Allow them to cool on the sheet (they'll be very crumbly when they first come out). Store in an airtight tin or tub.

Denver's Raisin Loaf

DENVER'S SWEET TOOTH doesn't go unnoticed, including by Lady Jones, who takes pity on the girl and her haunted family. She galvanizes the community into action so that food begins to appear on the doorstep of 124: a sack of white beans, a plate of cold rabbit meat, a basket of eggs.

And when Denver calls on her, Lady Jones bakes a raisin loaf (which seems to be her speciality) just for her, "since Denver was set on sweet things."

A swirl of cinnamon sugar adds extra sweetness to our loaf, which is wonderful sliced and eaten as it is or with a scraping of butter.

Makes 1 medium loaf

INGREDIENTS

½ cup (75 grams) soft brown sugar, divided, plus a little extra to sprinkle on top

2 teaspoons ground cinnamon, divided

3¼ cups (400 grams) all-purpose flour

⅔ cup (100 grams) raisins

2½ teaspoons yeast

1½ teaspoons salt

2 tablespoons (30 grams) butter, very soft

¾ cup (200 milliliters) milk, lukewarm, plus a little extra for brushing

METHOD

1. Place 2 tablespoons of the brown sugar and 1 teaspoon of the cinnamon in a small bowl. Mix and set aside. Combine the remaining dry ingredients (including the remaining brown sugar and cinnamon) in a large mixing bowl.

2. Make a well in the middle, add the butter, and slowly pour in the milk, mixing with a wooden spoon and then your hands (or you can use a stand mixer) until it comes away from the sides of the bowl.

3. Flour a surface and tip the dough out. Knead it to form a soft, smooth dough that no longer feels sticky. Grease the bowl and return the dough to it. Cover it with a tea towel and leave it to proof for 2 to 3 hours, until risen by around a third and noticeably puffy.

4. Grease a standard loaf pan (approximately 9.4 by 5 inches or 24 by 12 centimeters). On the floured surface, knock back the dough and shape it to roughly the length of the pan, then stretch and flatten it so it's more than twice the width. Sprinkle over the reserved cinnamon sugar, then roll up and tuck the dough into the pan, so the folded side is underneath.

5. Cover it again and allow it to rise for around another 2 hours, or until it's just peeping over the edge of the pan.

6. Preheat the oven to 350°F/180°C/160°C fan/gas mark 4. Brush the top of the loaf with milk and sprinkle with a little more sugar (if you're really set on sweet things).

7. Bake the loaf for around 45 minutes, or until golden brown on top and a wooden skewer inserted into the center comes out clean. Allow it to cool for around 10 minutes, then turn it out onto a wire rack to cool completely.

Washtub Full of Strawberry Shrug

Sethe can often be found cooking as if for a feast, kneading bread, stewing rutabaga (swede), sorting peas, and baking pies. It only highlights the loneliness of 124, a home chilled by the presence of a ghost. But the building once buzzed with (nonparanormal) activity, with a "feast for ninety people" held to celebrate Sethe's arrival with her newborn baby and Denver.

Along with pies, turkeys, batter bread, bread pudding, and mashed watermelon made into a punch is an intriguing "washtub full of strawberry shrug"—an alternative word for "shrub," sometimes known as drinking vinegar.

It's far lovelier and more refreshing than that suggests, with a tartness that balances the sweetness and makes for a satisfying drink simply served topped up with soda water to taste or used in a cocktail. Strawberry shrub works well with gin, in a twist on a Tom Collins, or vodka and soda.

Note: Because the fruit needs time to macerate and release its juices, you'll need to start preparation up to a week in advance of serving.

Makes 1 liter

INGREDIENTS

2½ to 3 cups (500 grams) strawberries, washed and hulled

Small handful of fresh mint leaves

2⅔ cups (500 grams) superfine sugar

2¼ cups (500 milliliters) red wine vinegar, plus a splash

METHOD

1. Halve the strawberries and place them in a large mixing bowl. Use a wooden spoon or potato masher to gently crush the berries and release a little of the juice.

2. Tear in the mint leaves and add the sugar, stirring to make sure it coats all of the fruit. Add a splash of red wine vinegar (this helps prevent fermentation) and stir again.

3. Cover and leave in a cool, dark place or the fridge for 2 to 3 days, stirring at least once a day, until it looks really juicy.

4. Strain it into another large bowl through a sieve, lightly pressing the fruit to get all the juice out. (You can save the fruit to make jam, compote, or ice cream or use in a dessert like trifle or summer pudding.)

5. Strain the liquid once more, through a muslin cloth, to get rid of any residue.

6. Add the vinegar, tasting as you go, until you're happy with the balance of tart and sweet. (You might not need to use all of it.)

7. Use a funnel to pour the liquid into sterilized, sealable bottles and store them in the fridge for 2 to 3 days for the flavors to settle. The shrug should keep well for at least a month after that.

Plum Cobbler

THIS CLASSIC DESSERT features in a pivotal scene in the novel, as Sethe's neighbors, led by Ella, unite to save her from the ghost that has taken over her world—and, perhaps, to exorcise demons of their own in the process. So they march on number 124, regaining their youth and strength with each stride. They imagine themselves scooping out potato salad as catfish sizzles and pops in a pan, and they see cobbler "oozing purple syrup" and staining their teeth.

A feature of tables in both England and the US, the cobbler is a little like a crumble, only with a lid of scone-like "cobbles" topping the fruit. We've used plums, though you could make this with other fruit like apples, pears, or berries.

Serves 6 to 8

INGREDIENTS

5½ cups (1 kilogram) plums, halved and stones removed

¾ cups (150 grams) light brown sugar

2 tablespoons sweet vermouth or water

3–4 sprigs fresh thyme

Topping

1¾ cups (200 grams) self-rising flour

Pinch of salt

⅓ cup (75 grams) butter, fridge cold and cubed

3 tablespoons superfine sugar

1 medium egg

2 tablespoons whole milk, plus a little extra for brushing

1 tablespoon brown sugar

Double cream or vanilla ice cream, to serve

METHOD

1. Preheat the oven to 390°F/200°C/180°C fan/gas mark 6. Place the plums in a 9-inch (23-centimeter) square ovenproof dish, sprinkle over the brown sugar, and toss together.

2. Drizzle over the vermouth and nestle the sprigs of thyme between the plums, spreading them evenly through the dish.

3. Pop in the oven for 10 to 15 minutes, until the fruit is softened but still holds its shape.

4. Meanwhile, to make the pastry, sift the flour and salt into a large bowl and rub the butter in with your fingertips to form a texture like coarse breadcrumbs. Add the sugar and loosely mix with your hands, making a well in the center.

5. In a small bowl beat together the egg and milk and pour into the well, mixing with a fork to form a rough dough.

6. Lightly flour a surface and turn out the dough. Knead it to form a smooth dough, then roll it out to around ¾ centimeter thick.

7. Using a 6-centimeter cutter, stamp out rounds, gathering the scraps and rerolling until you've used most of the dough.

8. Arrange these over the fruit (don't worry if there are gaps), brush with a little milk, and sprinkle with the brown sugar.

9. Pop in the oven for around 20 minutes, or until the topping is golden brown and lightly puffed up. Serve with double cream or a scoop of vanilla ice cream.

13

Domestic Vampires and Distant Memories of Food in Jewelle Gomez's *The Gilda Stories*

FOOD IS BUT A DISTANT MEMORY FOR THE GENRE-DEFYING CHARACTERS OF THIS GROUNDBREAKING NOVEL. A VAMPIRE'S LOVE OF CHAMPAGNE, HOWEVER, IS ETERNAL.

HUNGER IS NO stranger to the vampire story. Seeking out sustenance is, after all, the raison d'être of these immortal creatures, infamous for sucking blood and snuffing out lives. Quaffing champagne isn't quite so typical. Dreaming of a mother's biscuits, made with real butter, even less so.

A description of those biscuits (the American kind, puffed up and fluffy inside, designed to be split while warm) opens Jewelle Gomez's 1991 novel, a sapphic vampire tale that follows The Girl (later, Gilda) over two centuries from slavery in 1850 Louisiana to a postapocalyptic 2050. Food is interwoven with memory, rubbed down over time like butter into flour so that all that remains are jumbled-up crumbs, ready to be baked into something new again. From the start, it also marks this out as a very different brand of vampire—and Gothic—novel.

It's through food that The Girl remembers her mother. She wakes alone, having run away from the farm where she was enslaved, and imagines that the straw is her mother's tickles and pinches and that the cold, moldy smell of the dark, dank barn where she is hiding is the comforting "dough smell" of her parent. Later, asked about her family, she has the same sensory recall, describing "the smell of bread, shiny with butter, and the snow-white raw cotton tinged with blood from her fingers."

The domestic scene she recalls in the barn, conjuring the experience into her mind as an escape from present horror, is of a mother and daughter cooking together, the daughter proudly showing that she has managed to cook the gruel without it sticking to the pot and the mother indulging her with a brisk smile before dishing out the next task.

It isn't a typical domestic scene, though. This breakfast is not for them, or their family, but the people who own them. As in Toni Morrison's *Beloved*, food provides woefully insufficient pockets of comfort, and its enjoyment is in some ways heightened by the rarity of those moments but ultimately rotted by them.

Here, the biscuits tell of the inhumanity of the slave owners; they're too ignorant and "just barely human" to tell the difference between proper butter and pig fat. In a nod to what's to come, and the novel's vampiric theme, the mother tells The Girl that those people "suck up the world, don't taste it." They consume and destroy with bottomless greed but without joy and without savoring life and its simple pleasures (like flaky, buttery, doughy biscuits).

The actual vampires in this story, however, do the opposite. They taste or experience the world, and they draw blood without violence. As they feed, they also hold, soothe, and even nurture.

In her 2015 foreword to the novel, Gomez explains how it was born out of rage at female abasement and harassment. Gilda is the ultimate answer: "an escaped slave girl who becomes a vampire." She turns powerlessness into the ultimate power—over life and death—and bears witness to the depravity and cruelty of humanity over two hundred years.

Writing through a lens of "lesbian feminism," as Gomez describes it, and over such a broad sweep of time, allows her to expose human foibles and fallacies and to explore complex themes within a vampire story. Finding solutions to the biggest human problems (from the abuse of power to gender, racial, and class inequalities) requires, the author suggests, the breaking of the skin and the drawing of blood.

So a vampire novel was the perfect way to take this metaphor and run with it, joyously. Gomez's characters are likeable and imbued with human warmth. There's a contrast between the inescapable horrors associated with vampirism and the community these particular vampires have built, and maintained, over centuries. They travel, they enjoy each other's company, and they even sip champagne. Sorel, a more experienced vampire than Gilda when they meet in 1890, explains that most of the group have "no tolerance for food and drink," but all of his "children" enjoy champagne. It must, he jokes, be "in the blood."

Champagne is raised, clinked, and sipped throughout the novel, highlighting the vitality of the characters and, in a way, drawing our attention to the fact that they don't eat . . . food.

As with Mary Shelley's *Frankenstein*, these affable vampires challenge the concept, or construct, of Otherness and call into question who the real monster is here, exactly. They're hidden in plain sight, with Gilda taking advantage of the fact that she is already judged for her open lesbianism and her Blackness to disguise her real secret. They question society's stereotypes and inequalities and snatch away the ability to define ourselves in opposition to the monstrous Other, forcing us to face our own monstrosity instead.

Food, in a similar paradoxical fashion, is warm and unifying while also holding elements of monstrosity and representing a constant threat. As Gilda witnesses, time and time again, these vampires exercise more humanity than many humans do. They care for each other and share stories, often featuring increasingly distant and vague memories of food.

The descriptions become less detailed, from glazed biscuits, freshly turned out and still hot from the oven, to vague "memories of her mother's cooking years ago in Gulfport, Mississippi." Time is passing, and the memory of specific foods, tastes, and aromas is fading with it.

In 1950s Boston, Skip—the "youthful pimp" of Gilda's hairdressing salon client, Savannah—promises an "old-fashion-down-home recipe spaghetti with fried chicken tomato sauce," bubbling away and releasing aromas of tomatoes and garlic. The latter, and especially Skip's mention of garlic bread, draws wry looks between Bird and Gilda. Skip is puzzled; as readers, we're in on the joke, and the reference to a vampiric stereotype only serves to highlight that these are not your stereotypical vampires.

Even their "victims" are often more like companions, treated with warmth and compassion and, with Gilda in particular, forming a bond we might associate more with people sitting around a table and sharing a meal. She meets many on her epic voyage through time, through the horrors of slavery to moments of indescribably joyous freedom, otherwise beyond human reach.

Gilda is still a vampire, with the bloodlust of her predecessors, though she draws blood in exchange for warmth and a sense of belonging. She was brought into this immortal world in the same way, nurtured and fed by Bird—first with food ("corn pudding or a rabbit she had killed") and, later, her own blood, delivered from her chest in a scene rich in maternal imagery.

These are domestic vampires—vampires with the closeness of a tightly knit family but a family that has chosen to be one. As they clink champagne glasses, slowly sip wine, prepare plates of sweet yams (for nonvampiric loved ones), and dream of biscuits from the distant past, Gomez's infinitely likeable characters turn the vampire genre—along with stereotypes around race and sexuality—on its head.

Real Butter Biscuits with Gravy

THE CONNECTION BETWEEN food—its tastes, textures, and aromas—and memory is powerful, and there's something especially evocative about baked goods. Perhaps it's a connection to childhood, as with The Girl, who imagines her mother's biscuits in a moment of terror.

Our American-style biscuits are served with a thick, creamy, peppery gravy with sausage meat and mushrooms, for a satisfying dish that's typically eaten for breakfast or brunch but is certainly hearty enough for supper. You can use any sausages, including vegetarian ones, or you can skip the meat completely and double the quantity of mushrooms.

In another nod to the book, we've also finished ours with butter—just as The Girl's Mama did—to "make 'em shine."

This recipe serves four as a complete meal, though could equally stretch to serve eight as part of a bigger breakfast or brunch spread.

Serves 4 as a main or up to 8 as a side

INGREDIENTS

Biscuits

¾ cup (200 milliliters) buttermilk or whole milk

Squeeze of lemon juice (if using whole milk)

1¾ (200 grams) self-rising flour

¼ teaspoon baking soda

1 tablespoon superfine sugar

¼ teaspoon salt

⅓ cup (75 grams) butter, fridge cold and cubed, divided

Gravy

6–8 sausages (approximately 350 grams of sausages), meat or vegetarian

2 tablespoons olive oil

1½ to 2 cups (150 grams) mushrooms, finely chopped

2 tablespoons all-purpose flour

Slightly over 2 cups (500 milliliters) milk

½ teaspoon cayenne pepper
Salt and freshly ground pepper

METHOD

1. If using whole milk, make a buttermilk substitute by pouring the milk into a jug and adding the lemon juice. Cover and set aside for around 10 minutes, or until it starts to thicken and smells slightly sour. Stir and set it aside.

2. Preheat the oven to 390°F/200°C/180°C fan/gas mark 6. Sift the flour, baking soda, sugar, and salt into a large mixing bowl.

3. Set aside around one-fifth of the butter and add the rest to the bowl. Using your fingertips, rub it into the dry ingredients to form a texture like fine breadcrumbs.

4. Make a well in the center and pour in the buttermilk, a little at a time, mixing with a wooden spoon or your hands.

5. Flour a surface and tip out the dough. Knead it lightly until smooth (it will still be a little sticky). Sprinkle with more flour and, using your hands, flatten it to around 2.5 centimeters thick and stamp out rounds with an 8-centimeter cutter. Gather up the scraps and repeat until you've used most of the dough. You should get 8 to 10 rounds.

6. Line a baking sheet with parchment paper and place the rounds on it. Bake for around 10 minutes, while you make the gravy.

7. To make the gravy, if using sausages that have a skin, score down the length and squeeze out the meat onto a board. Roughly chop. If using vegetarian sausages, roughly chop into small pieces.

8. Heat the oil in a large frying pan, add the sausage meat, and gently fry over medium heat for around 5 minutes, or until no pink bits remain.

9. Add the mushrooms and continue to cook until they have released their water and started to brown a little.

10. Add the flour and give everything a good mix to combine, then gradually add the milk, stirring continuously.

11. Keep stirring for 3 to 4 minutes, until the sauce starts to thicken, then add the cayenne, season to taste, and remove from the heat.

12. When the biscuits are ready, nicely risen and pale golden in color, remove them from the oven and, while they're still hot, place a little of the remaining butter on top of each one. Leave them to one side until you've finished the gravy but try to keep them warm.

13. Once everything's ready, split the biscuits and divide them between four plates, spoon the gravy over the top, and serve.

Old-Fashion-Down-Home Spaghetti

One of Skip's specialities is his "old-fashion-down-home recipe spaghetti with fried chicken tomato sauce," packed with garlic and herbs. Aside from being a wry reference to vampiric folklore (and a certain aversion to garlic), his dish sounds pretty delicious. Re-create it with this suitably spicy arrabbiata, which is infused with a subtle warmth thanks to the whole chile that spreads its heat as the sauce simmers. You can adjust the heat level by choosing hotter or milder chiles and by chopping up more or less of it to throw back into the sauce.

Just as Skip did, we're topping this with leftover fried chicken (or a vegan alternative)—though you can also buy a package especially for the recipe.

Serves 2

INGREDIENTS

Arrabbiata Sauce

3 tablespoons olive oil

½ onion, diced

1 medium red chile

3 cloves garlic, finely chopped

1⅔ cups (400 grams) canned chopped tomatoes

1 17-ounce (500-gram) carton passata

1 tablespoon ketchup or tomato purée

½ teaspoon black pepper

Pinch of salt

8.8 ounces (250 grams) fried chicken or vegan substitute, leftovers or store-bought

Spaghetti, to serve

Handful of fresh basil

METHOD

1. Start by making the arrabbiata sauce. Place the oil in a medium saucepan over medium heat, then add the onion and cook gently for 6 to 7 minutes, until soft but not browned.

2. Pierce the chile a few times with a sharp knife. Add it to the pan along with the garlic and fry for a further 1 to 2 minutes.

3. Pour in the tomatoes, passata, ketchup, pepper, and salt and give it a good stir. Cover the pan with a lid and cook over low heat for half an hour, stirring occasionally.

4. Meanwhile, slice the fried chicken into strips, then warm through in the microwave or fry with a little oil in a pan over low heat for just a few minutes. If using store-bought, cook according to package instructions and slice. It's delicious cold, but if you want it to be warm, time it so it's ready at the same time as the sauce and spaghetti.

5. Meanwhile, cook the spaghetti according to package instructions (again, timing it so it's ready at roughly the same time as the sauce and chicken).

6. Remove the lid from the sauce and carefully fish out the chile. Finely chop the flesh and add some or all to the sauce, with or without the seeds, depending on how hot you like it. (Taste as you go.)

7. Add the cooked spaghetti to the pot and stir so it's nicely covered. Tear the basil leaves and add to the sauce, stirring again.

8. Divide the spaghetti between two bowls, top with the fried chicken, and serve.

A Pretty Mean Garlic Bread

While his pasta sauce is bubbling away, almost violently threatening to overspill the pan, Skip curses himself; he's forgotten to buy some Italian bread to make his other speciality, "a pretty mean garlic bread." Again, the vampires share a knowing glance at this ingredient—though Skip, of course, isn't in on the joke.

Once you've tried this simple recipe, packed with roasted garlic, sun-dried tomatoes, and rosemary, you'll never need (or want) to buy Italian bread again.

Serves 6 to 8

INGREDIENTS

1 bulb garlic
Olive oil, for brushing

Dough

1½ cups (350 milliliters) lukewarm water
2 teaspoons dried yeast
3¾ cups (500 grams) bread flour
2 teaspoons fine salt
5 tablespoons olive oil, divided, plus extra for greasing
8–10 small sprigs rosemary
3–4 sun-dried tomatoes, chopped
1 teaspoon flaked sea salt, to sprinkle on top

METHOD

1. Preheat the oven to 350°F/180°C/160°C fan/gas mark 4. Slice the top off the bulb of garlic (so the tops of the cloves are just exposed) and, using your fingers, gently rub away any excess paper from the skin. Brush with a little olive oil, wrap in foil, and roast for 40 to 45 minutes, until tender. Set aside to cool.

2. To make the dough, place the water in a small bowl, add the yeast, stir, and leave for a couple of minutes, until it starts to bubble.

3. Sift the flour into a large mixing bowl, add the salt, and stir.

4. Take the cooled garlic and, using your fingers, squeeze out the cloves. Add these to the flour and stir.

5. Make a well in the center, add 2 tablespoons of the oil, and slowly add the water and yeast mixture, stirring with a wooden spoon to form a sticky dough.

6. Flour a surface and, using floured hands, transfer the dough. Knead until it forms a smooth, just slightly sticky dough—you can add a little more flour as you go.

7. Set aside to proof for 2 to 3 hours, until puffy and risen by around a third.

8. Brush a medium, deep-sided baking sheet with oil, place the dough in the center, and stretch and flatten with your hands so it fills the pan. Cover the pan with a tea towel and leave to proof for a further hour or so.

9. Preheat the oven to 430°F/220°C/200°C fan/gas mark 7. Make dimples in the risen dough, drizzle over the remaining 3 tablespoons olive oil, and push the rosemary sprigs and sun-dried tomatoes into the holes.

10. Sprinkle with the salt and bake for 20 to 25 minutes, until golden on top. Cut into slices and serve warm. (It'll keep for a few days, wrapped up, but is best warmed before serving.)

Fearless French 75

LIKE DRACULA, GILDA and her cohorts "do not sup." They do, however, sip, drinking champagne so regularly that you might say it runs in their blood.

There are plenty of sparkling cocktails to choose from, including the classic champagne cocktail made with just a sugar cube, Angostura bitters, and (obviously) fizz. But we think the French 75 would get the vampires' approval.

Believed to have been invented in the early twentieth century, on the cusp of the 1920 Prohibition laws, it feels like an appropriately illicit and potent drink for our vampires to be sipping. It's named after a 75-millimeter gun used by the French army during the First World War, and it's suitably lethal. And, like Gilda, the story of the French 75 spans several eras, with the cocktail changing over time yet still retaining its steely character.

Today, you're more likely to be served the sherbet-like mix of lemon juice, sugar, gin, and champagne, while the earliest versions were laced with apple brandy and turned blood-red with grenadine. Ours is a hybrid, topped up with fizz to mimic the effervescence of life freshly imbibed. . . .

Serves 1

INGREDIENTS

1 tablespoon dry gin

1 tablespoon Calvados or other apple brandy

½ tablespoon grenadine syrup

Squeeze of lemon juice

½ cup (125 milliliters) champagne or other sparkling wine

METHOD

1. Fill a pint glass or cocktail shaker with ice and add all the ingredients except the champagne.

2. Stir with a long bar spoon for around 30 seconds, so it's well combined and chilled by the ice.

3. Strain into a coupe or flute and top with the champagne (tilting the glass and pouring slowly so the blood doesn't escape too quickly).

Afterword

What to Read Next

If our spooky cookbook has you hungry for more (and we hope it has), there's still plenty to explore at the intersection of food and Gothic literature.

Here are just a few of our favorite texts that use food in a deliciously dark (or, perhaps, darkly delicious) way to hint at horrors, cast shade on characters, or evoke a sense of queasy uneasiness in the reader. Bon appétit!

"Rappaccini's Daughter" (1844), Nathaniel Hawthorne

An early example of edible imagery in Gothic literature, Hawthorne's short story focuses on a girl who resides in a lush garden—the product of her father's botanical experiments. As a young scholar, and would-be suitor, enters the picture, edible flowers, herbs, and shrubs turn poisonous as love turns into envy.

"The Cask of Amontillado" (1846), Edgar Allan Poe

Poe's short story is a chilling tale of deception, revenge—and the allure of wine, specifically, the rare and enticing Amontillado, a sherry that serves as the intoxicating catalyst for the story's sinister plot.

Wuthering Heights (1847), Emily Brontë

One aspect of *Wuthering Heights* has received little attention from critics: the food. The brooding characters aren't exactly eating, drinking, and being merry. Instead, the food reflects the depth of sadness. So hands are plunged into porridge, and miserable meals include gruel and dry toast.

Bleak House (1852-1853), Charles Dickens

Dickens masterfully weaves a culinary thread through his biting satirical novel, initially luring readers with delightful depictions of gastronomic pleasures, only to later employ these same descriptions as weapons against the characters. This is strikingly exemplified through descriptions of unappetizing raw food given to vulnerable, severely neglected children.

The Edible Woman (1969), Margaret Atwood

Atwood's novel, set during the early feminist movement of the 1960s, follows the life of Marian McAlpin, who increasingly feels she is being eaten up by a patriarchal society. Her fears manifest themselves in an inability to eat, as her relationship with food becomes as unhealthy as her relationships with the men who threaten to consume her.

The Vegetarian (2007), Han Kang

Food plays a central role in Kang's narrative, acting as a powerful symbol of rebellion and transformation. The protagonist's decision to become a vegetarian is not merely a dietary choice—it's a means of asserting her agency and breaking free from societal expectations.

The Little Stranger (2009), Sarah Waters

Hundreds Hall is a very hungry house indeed. This book, set in the aftermath of the Second World War, handles difficult themes with the gentle touch of a ghost. Teatimes are traumatic and often terrifying, while a cocktail party descends into hellish scenes.

The Confessions of Frannie Langton (2019), Sara Collins

Collins's novel follows the story of Frannie Langton, a Jamaican-born maid in nineteenth-century London who is accused of murder. Reading and food are intertwined, from the scene where Frannie is forced to eat pages of a book as punishment to the description of consuming a novel as like imbibing a long, warm drink.

Mexican Gothic (2020), Silvia Moreno-García

Moreno-García's story plays with the idea of ghosts and haunting, casting light (and shadows) on colonialism. It all leads up to a monstrous and highly gratifying revelation that hinges on ... mushrooms! Along the way, food—so often a source of comfort and a sense of belonging—evokes loneliness and displacement.

Acknowledgments

TO THOSE WHO believed in *A Gothic Cookbook* as much as we did.

To every single person who bought a copy before it even existed.

To our social media followers and online community, who shouted loudly and proudly about our project (and helped us to reach our funding target).

To all our friends and family who helped with the testing (and tasting) of recipes, from the "experimental" stage to the little details.

To Goths, literature lovers, and food fanatics around the world . . .

THANK YOU!

About the Authors

ELLA BUCHAN is an experienced journalist and editor specializing in food and travel and with a penchant for the darker things in life. Her writing has been published in the *Times, National Geographic Traveler FOOD,* the *Independent*, and others. Born in Newcastle upon Tyne, England, and now settled by the coast just outside the city, she has a First-Class bachelor's degree in English literature—and a WSET level 3 (advanced) qualification in wines. *A Gothic Cookbook* perfectly marries her passions for writing, literature, and food, all in one deliciously dark package.

DR. ALESSANDRA PINO is an expert on the intersections of the Gothic, food, and cultural memory. Born in Hampstead, London, to an Italian mother and Venezuelan diplomat father, Alessandra grew up in different countries and a cross cultures and languages. She holds degrees from "L'Orientale" University, Naples (Italy), and the University of Westminster (UK; MA in translation studies); she was awarded a PhD in food, cultural memory, and the Gothic in 2022. Alessandra worked with a Michelin-starred chef for nearly ten years before moving to academia, researching, and publishing on food, cultural memory, the supernatural, and the Gothic.

LEE HENRY is a freelance illustrator and graphic designer based in North East England. With a background in editorial and publishing, he has worked with leading brands such as BBC Good Food, the *Radio Times*, and *Where Magazine*. He provides specialist food and drink branding and design via his agency, Ounce Of Style. His unique illustrations combine intricate hand-drawn line work with digital color elements and are influenced by his love of food, travel, and jazz music.

Index

Andrews McMeel Publishing
a division of Andrews McMeel Universal
1130 Walnut Street, Kansas City, Missouri 64106
www.andrewsmcmeel.com

24 25 26 27 28 VEP 10 9 8 7 6 5 4 3 2 1

ISBN: 978-1-5248-9408-5

Library of Congress Control Number: 2024938590

Editor: Katie Gould
Production Editor: Jennifer Straub
Production Manager: Julie Skalla

First published in 2024 by Unbound

Unbound
c/o TC Group, 6th Floor King's House, 9-10 Haymarket, London SW1Y 4BP
www.unbound.com